Other works by S. D. Warnsley

Onyx-I Am No Hero

The

SUNDARIAN

E A R T H

By

S. D. Warnsley

The Sundarian
Earth

Cover and Interior Design by Heather UpChurch
www.artanddesignstudios.net

Copyright © 2016

Publisher Musicorp Publishing

Library of Congress 2016900303
ISBN 978-0-9971068-0-0
Ebook 978-0-9971068-1-7

Author S. D. Warnsley

Dedicated to H. M. Warnsley

For allowing me to be creative. For your kindness and devotion, and for your endless support.

Thanks for always being there for me.

CHAPTER ONE

The yellow-red sun has gradually vanished and the bright pale-white moon is making its way into atmospheric view. Night lay over the calm desert, enveloping the United States Military Communications Facility in silent darkness.

A cool, gentle wind flows over the desert. Only the diminutive night creatures, those shunning the day and the sun's blistering heat moved with ease in the coolness.

Four guards patrolled the outside perimeters of the building, which secretly housed some of the country's crucial communication equipment.

The airspace was guarded by a lofty tower connected directly to the square block structure. Two lookouts kept minuscule vigilance from the three-story guard post.

As the guards rotate for their night rounds, and with one guard binocular trained on a few straggly coyotes in the desert distance, an unmarked assault Hummer charged brazenly up the sole road leading to the closed gates.

The black fortified grill of the Hummer smashed through the heavy gates, ripping the barricades off their hinges, and lurched to a stop at the building's side door.

Six black-clad figures leaped out of the vehicle. All were armed over their snug black fatigues and baldrics of personal artillery.

Five muscled men and one sylphlike woman swiftly took in the surroundings.

"Ok. Let move, we know what we are here for" says Mystic looking at the facility.

Among them were two mammoth Toroks, Kelvar and Zevyn, invaders from the planet Toria intent on enslaving Earth. The Toroks, seven feet tall, strappingly thick with full black bushy hair that extends down to their shoulders; they are wearing their protective body armor made for warfare from their home planet Toria under their black fatigues. The other three men and single woman each had their own mental ax to grind against their home civilization, each superior to the ordinary man, and each skilled in their individual specialties.

Demolisher is strong-built and brimming with uranium-enhanced skin and exceptional strength. He grinned at several guards that rounded the building. Polar shared his enthusiasm, but the desert heat, even at night, annoyed him.

The deadly Wraith Blade, the only female of the group, took half a step back, the belts crossing her chest jammed with kunai knives. At her back was a pair of lethal razor sharp blades. She already held twin wakizashi blades, blades glinting in the moonlight.

Mystic, the least armed, watched his friends alacrity with an attentive eye.

"Stop where you are, now!" one of the guards yelled as he ran up on the invaders, drawing his pistol.

Before the desert-camo clad guard could finish the movement, Demolisher clubbed him with a powerful swipe of one arm. He turned to the next guard and sprung, flattening him with a double-punch to the chest. Sternum agonizingly cracking, the guard fell, clutching his chest and moaning.

Kelvar and Zevyn, the Toroks, headed for the door as two more zealous guards burst from around the building.

Kelvar aimed his pulse canon and fired at them. The fierce surge of energy burst through the air causing incredible destruction to the side of the building, instantly throwing the soldiers backwards, discombobulating their senses, and they fell to the ground, confused, burned, and half-blind.

Without waiting, Demolisher dashed to the building's thick door and roughly crashed it open with a single heave of his shoulder.

He tore the door off its hinges and flung it behind him. Without missing a beat, the others followed him inside.

The building sectioned off immediately into a hallway, dimly lit and well-guarded. Demolisher went first, bulldozing his way through the first three guards that attempted firing on them. He left them on the floor, unconscious, and led Polar, Mystic, the Toroks, and Wraith Blade on. Collectively they were known as Chaos, and together they were unstoppable.

They headed down the corridor.

It was an elongated maze of rooms secured behind locked doors. Polar froze the first door with cold blast from his hands, and it shattered under the frigidly high temperatures. Its brittle shards scattered to the floor.

Behind the open doorway was a maze of spare uniforms, but it wasn't what the group sought.

They moved on and stopped at the next door that shielded a raucous buzz of technology and Demolisher shattered it. The telecommunications supply room opened to them. The surprised guard to the right of the room drew his pistol, but Demolisher crushed him with a single forceful blow to the face. The guard unconsciously crumpled to the floor.

Zevyn looked greedily around the room, gaze drifting over the equipment.

Polar and Mystic had already moved to the next room that housed the security systems. They hastily disabled the lone guard that tried to stop them. At the consoles they punched in the computer codes to shut down the alarms and security cameras, effectively hiding their mission.

Wraith Blade stood at the open doorway of the telecommunication supply room, watching the lights in the control systems room blink out. She grinned at Polar and Mystic's success, her dark, sharp eyes on the hallway as the Toroks worked in the telecommunication supply room behind her. Her lithe form belied smooth reflexes and cunningly honed talents ranging from edged weapons to expert marksmanship. Her long, curly brunette hair cascaded around a lovely but lethal face, framing eyes that could both haunt and hate with equal passion.

"Got it," Zevyn said, plucking something from one of the shelves lining the wall. He put it in his bag and slung it over his shoulder and tightened the strap across his chest.

A scamper down the hall made Wraith Blade's attention flick there. Three guards rushed down the corridor, yelling into their shoulder radios as they drew their pistols.

She sprinted forward to engage them. Blade flashing, she sliced through the first guard, nearly halving him from hip to opposite shoulder before he could even scream. She spun and sent a high-kick to the second man's chest. He tried to grab her foot, but she slashed his forearm with the second short sword. It flung off, spattering a wall with blood before falling with a sickening thud to the floor.

The third guard fired pointblank at her face, but she quickly pivoted, dodging the bullet, and then leapt to one side wall and pushed off to land behind him. With an expert slice of her sword that had earned her notoriety in several Chinese provinces, her left wakizashi slashed open his spine. He cried out in terrible agony, falling to his knees, trying to crawl away.

She took her time stepping up to his writhing body and delivered a quick slash across the back of his neck. He fell limp.

"Too messy," a voice rumbled down the hallway.

She gradually looked up to see Polar.

"You and your knives," he grunted as she moved past the guard on the floor. "Hurry up. This place makes my blood boil."

She stopped and held the reddened tip of one short blade between their faces, smiling mockingly. "Not a knife, Polar. "Blades."

She walked back to the telecommunications supply room.

"You're as finicky as a feline," he grumbled, following, frowning at the menagerie of knives and the longer katana and jian strapped across her back.

She tossed a look over her shoulder. "Don't taunt the blades."

He mumbled something she didn't hear as they went to join the Toroks in the small room. He hadn't exaggerated too much when he'd complained about his blood boiling. He hadn't always been known as Polar; he'd once been Stanley Bennett, assistant to a negligent professor who'd been in charge of a bio-chemical research study in Norway's arctic. That negligence led to Bennett's exposure to a toxic gas called Nitroglesine that evacuated the facility. The bitter cold of the Norwegian arctic had reacted with his body's chromosomes, altering his physiology and enabling him to produce freezing temperatures from his hands at will. Most of the other evacuees assumed Bennett dead. He wasn't, but the changed Bennett was now Polar.

Another burst of guards rushed into the hallway through the doorway where Demolisher had ripped off the door. The two tower guards drew their weapons, taking quick beads on the raiders. Two green laser site lines zipped over the floor and to Wraith Blade's forehead.

Before a trigger could be squeezed, Mystic stepped from the controls room and held up his hand gesturing to the pair of guards. "Umbra!"

The guards turned ashen black, thin as their shadows, and slipped to the floor, rifles clattering beside them.

A chill swept over Wraith Blade and even Polar felt the uncanny use of the black arts.

"Now that's cold," Polar said, chuckling.

Mystic smirked at them and turned to the technology room. "How long?"

The two Toroks met them in the hallway. "All ready. The mainframe is loaded."

Demolisher came up the corridor from behind Polar and Wraith Blade. "Everyone's subdued" he said confidently.

A sudden screech of tires and brakes from outside was followed by a man shouting orders.

"More are coming," Kelvar said eyes on the open doorway.

"Get them!" the man's deep voice ordered from the outside grounds. "Every man to position! Don't let them leave this facility!"

Chaos looked to each other, silently agreeing on their plan. As one, they darted from the building and into the yard.

Two USMC Hummers and eight brawny soldiers in military garb faced them. With a yell native to their Torian homeland, Kelvar and Zevyn brandished their power lance staffs. Each triggered the retractable blades in their sword staffs and bellowed again, charging the soldiers.

A hail of bullets riveted the building's exterior as the reserve guards fired their automatic weapons.

Polar extended both arms, frost quickly formed on his hands, and he shot spiky freezing ice darts in return, downing two guards. Beside him, Demolisher grabbed the door he'd wrenched off earlier and heaved it at the commander.

With a shocked curse, the officer folded under the heavy door. He squirmed, trying to unpin himself from the quarter-ton door.

The guards repositioned, night-goggles pinpointing the Chaos members. They fell in behind the Hummers and one launched a grenade at Chaos.

Demolisher's body blocked the grenade, it exploded. He stepped before Wraith Blade, taking the brunt of the next volley of bullets. They peppered off his hardened skin, ricocheting back at the shooters. Wraith Blade has taken out the jian blade from its scabbard at her back and raised it, stepping around Demolisher's protection. She expertly deflected the few bullets still pelting her, the lead ringing off the blade, sparking in the night. She spun two knives from the belt crossing her chest and flung them with precision aim.

Both knives found their marks, depositing in the throats of the Marines looking around one of the Hummers. They gasped, grabbed at their bloody necks, and fell to their knees.

The Toroks had already taken down two other soldiers and were moving on to the next pair. One marine guard managed to throw grenades at Chaos.

Wraith Blade rushed the marine with the blade and cleaved the nearest in half. Mystic stepped from the rubble as the rest of Chaos ducked at the noise of the exploding grenades.

The entirely bald and clean shaven, Mystic arts master held up both hands again gesturing slowly and shouted above the noise and smoke. "Terga dare!"

The remaining soldiers and both Hummers were blown back by an invisible force of a powerful wind, lifting them and flinging them backwards, landing violently against the chain link fence surrounding the facility. Even the commander was scooped up and deposited, the building door crushing into one of the Hummer doors.

The dust settled, replaced by painful moans and the soldiers, all wounded, cursing lowly as they tried to disengage from the Hummers.

Both Toroks nodded at Mystic's work. The former Queens resident hadn't shared too much about his background with the rest of Chaos, but they did know he'd seen his parents killed before his eyes by corrupt Lexington Park city policemen. As a boy, Mystic, then Daniel Everson, hadn't understood the politics behind the police frame-up, nor could he do anything to stop them. He had, however, taken matters into his own hands and pursued Mystic arts magic, and ultimately, the powerful amulet known as the Opal Stone. It led him to form Chaos.

"We've got what we came for," Kelvar said, looking to Zevyn, who nodded, lifting the shoulder under his bag strap. Kelvar glanced to the others. "Let's go!"

Demolisher gave the fallen guards a final glimpse and seemingly with little effort, turned over the lone Hummer that was still on its blown tires. The vehicle fell, trapping three guards under it. Demolisher grinned and turned away. The mammoth figure, a man once known as Michael Owens around the Stanton Pennsylvania train's shipyard, walked away from the metal and bodily carnage he'd wrought. Polar stands looking at the last visible guards and marines, briskly shooting ice darts at any who comes into view.

Chaos swiftly loaded back into their Hummer and left the wounded communications facility. Total devastation had taken less than seven minutes.

After some time, the emergency rescue medics begin to arrive at the facility. Moments later another vehicle entered the smoldering area. A Jeep with two men in it skidded to a stop. The darkened windows zipped down.

Inside, Global Security Alliance agent Devante Marcelle and a well-inclined and talented student named David Ramirez gawked at the destruction. The building was severely damaged, fires were burning, and the gates were crashed and the fencing half-folded on one side. At that fold were the two Hummers, each still pinning a few guards. A military ambulance, no lights flashing, was parked near the wreckage of men and vehicles.

Global Security Alliance agent Marcelle with his low military style haircut, and boyish looks, and exceptionally compassionate eyes surveyed the area with dreaded astonishment.

Ramirez, having the timeless young attractive Latino male look, also looked to the scorched building, and then around for the door that appeared to have been blown off. He found it near the Hummers. By it lay the commander, injured and unconscious as he was attended by medics. "They blew the building from inside?"

Marcelle turned off the ignition. "Not according to our preliminary reports. It was ripped off by one of the assailants." He scowled over the damage. Nothing about this made in the least sense to him. He flipped his jacket lapel under his GSA identification badge and snapped it, showing the ID.

Beside him, Ramirez did the same over his less-than-official associate tag.

Marcelle opened his door. "Let's go find out what happened here."

More medical emergency personal was starting to arrive. They got out of the Jeep and cautiously made their way across the cinder-strewn gravel to the doorway that gaped hollowly into the once well-guarded communications facility. One of the two remaining guards looked crossly to them inside, hand at his sidearm.

"Global Security Alliance Agent Devante Marcelle." He flashed his GSA badge. "He's with me."

The guard looked to the badge for a long moment in the poor light, eyes flicking between the two men. "All right," he finally said. "Go ahead, but watch your step. It's a mess inside."

Marcelle nodded to him and stepped into the building's main corridor.

"It is a mess," Ramirez said in disbelief.

Before them stood the aftermath of Chaos' destructive visit.

The walls were singed and deep black, and in some places around the doorframes were an odd gray, pocked appearance that permeated the metal framing. Marcelle stopped at the first doorway, studying the small circle markings. They looked as if tiny bubbles had popped, leaving the pockmarks.

"Coming through!" a medic called.

Both Marcelle and Ramirez moved to one side of the hallway as several medics carried a gurney past them. It was followed by two more. Each form was covered by a blanket soaked with red in several spots.

"Hold it," Marcelle said, pulling back the blanket on the first body as the medics paused.

Below the blanket, the dead guard's body was prone. His desert fatigues were ripped open with a single slice down his back, exposing the vertebrae below. A dark patch of deep red was at the nape of his neck, hair matted with blood. Marcelle covered the body.

"My God," he said, in disbelief. The injuries were signatory of a once-familiar face. He looked grimly to the other gurneys as they passed. It was clear that no one had survived those blades.

He turned to see Ramirez with a cell phone to his ear.

"...but that's what it looks like here." Ramirez said loudly to the caller. He hung up and turned his attention to the doorframes. "The preliminary metallurgy reports came in on the metal doors. It's similar to the missiles facility."

Marcelle continued down the hallway, glancing into each of the small rooms as they passed them. Most were untouched, but at the supply room he stopped. It had been rifled, a few items scattered, but mostly it was a selective search. "What do they report?"

"The metal scrapings from the lab that were taken from the pocked doorframes and shreds of door from the floor show rapid freezing and blunt force trauma."

Marcelle looked to him. "They were frozen and then smashed?"

Ramirez shook his head. "Frozen to such cold temperatures that the individual alloys were made brittle. Like the opposite of steel tempering; past tempering, like a sword blade."

Marcelle decline to look back at the last gurney being carried out of the building. "I get it."

Ramirez nodded to the supply room. "Not much is missing."

"Enough is missing." Marcelle shifted his attention from the shelves in the room to the younger man. Despite all that David Ramirez added to the FBI and GSA's investigations, he was still a college student. "We have to find a way to stop them. This is the second such attack and it's getting out of hand. They're pulverizing military facilities without batting an eye or leaving casualties of their own, and we don't know yet what they're after."

"I can't even piece together their plans by their patterns." Ramirez put his hand on his chin, shaking his head at the supply room. "First a missile facility, now a communications facility; what could they want?"

Marcelle continued down the hallway. "They're planning something disastrous." He gestured with one arm to the blood-spattered walls amid the crashed doors and pocked frames. "Just look at the firepower they have."

"We need to get this information back to the FBI." Ramirez didn't like the red dripping down the walls. "There are anomalies here that don't match the usual terrorist group attack MO's."

"I need to have all the surveillance footage of this attack," Ramirez said stiffly. "I'm going to appoint and mobilize a Special Forces unit."

"How long do you think we can keep this from the press?" Ramirez knew it was something that would be made public; it was only a matter of time.

Marcelle stopped at the telecommunications room where the instruments had been disabled. He shook his head. "I hope long enough for us to catch them."

"Have you got any new Intel on those missiles that went missing from the military supply plant?" Ramirez gave the room a brief study.

"Two missiles were stolen, long range capabilities. The military had a tracking device installed on each." Marcelle's tone grew more serious. "Whoever stole it removed the tracking devices. I don't know where those missiles are now."

Ramirez pulled out a standard compact camera and set the flash for the brightest setting. "I'll begin getting photos. I guess I'll start here. It looks like it was a focal point."

Marcelle nodded and knelt to carefully set his fingerprint dusting kit on the floor, not wanting to disturb anything in the security room. "I'll dust for fingerprints, but something tells me this was done by someone way past that. Rather, more than one someone."

"Who could have caused this much damage to a fortified facility?" Devante thinks to himself, "such destruction, we don't have the military capability to stop them. These are not your general terrorist organizations that I pursue around the world; these guys are much more implacable."

Ramirez snapped a few shots of the room from the doorway before delicately making his way in. "I don't think they're a smalltime terrorist group. I think these guys are getting ready to do something big. No gunfire from them. No hostages, just in and out with complete devastation following them."

Marcelle glanced to the few men coming down the hallway. They were the typical top brass military officials, ready to respond to the attack, just like at the missile location. And, he knew, they'd say as little as possible to actually help; they'd be too interested in covering for the military's responsibility in such a situation. Damage control, Marcelle knew.

"I'm meeting the regional brass now." He turned to greet the officers as Ramirez continued taking photos. "Back in a minute."

Later that night, Chaos reached their abandoned-looking warehouseon the outskirts of the hub of Lexington Park City. It was fully powered, but the vast windows were painted-over, so any passersby didn't give it a second look.

No one would have guessed what went on there, and if any visitor had happened to peek inside the building, it would have been their last look at anything.

Mystic drove the Hummer directly into the warehouse's open bay door garage and quickly clicked it shut behind them with the remote control; silently their deed blended into the tranquil night.

Within moments they were all out, minus Wraith Blade, who'd insisted on being let out several blocks away. Mystic lifted the vehicle's back hatch, smiling wickedly at the stolen goods.

While they began removing their black fatigue one piece jumpers, "Let's unpack and get this going," he said, tossing a bag to Kelvar.

The Torok caught it and heaved the strap onto his shoulder.

"Like candy from a baby," Demolisher said. He turned and headed for the opposite side of the warehouse. Demolisher, Polar, and Mystic did not take much time getting out of their black-clad suits then went directly to their tasks.

"Everything went perfect. We were in and out before they even knew what hit them," Kelvar said. "One-hundred percent perfect."

The warehouse had been especially selected for their needs; close enough to the city without being under any authority's watchful eye, isolated enough for easy coming and going. The upper levels were mostly collapsed, giving the building a condemned look, but the first two floors were solid and serviceable.

The far side of the floor had a menagerie of piece-meal but top of the line computers set up. Well-worn desk chairs and a few sofas rounded out the set of furniture, but what the décor lacked in finesse it made up for in blunt power.

Demolisher sat in one of these chairs and flexed his fingers, poised over the keyboard, eyes on the computer screen as it snapped to attention. He deftly tapped out a few commands.

"We now have money to finish repairs on the shuttle," Zevyn said, lowering his bag to the floor in the center of the sofas and other furniture. "Now we can start setting up the communications devices."

Demolisher's attention was on the lines of coordinates flashing across the computer screen.

Mystic watched from behind his chair. "So close."

One of the upper level doors opened, announcing someone's entry with a creak. A moment later, Wraith Blade dropped from the two stories' loft through a hole near one corner. She landed lightly, with superb agile grace, and walked over to join them.

"Took the scenic tour, did you?" Zevyn asked, eyeing her.

"I stayed behind to see if the military had any people follow us." She said confidently. "We were not followed. Everything is all clear."

"Good, Wraith Blade," he said. "Mystic, I have the protocols for the shuttle." He tossed a disc to Mystic standing near Demolisher. "You can start on those."

Mystic turned the disc over carefully, examining it as carefully as he did any new piece of information. "These military sequences should help with the configurations."

Polar glanced around at the rest of them. "The Toroks and I are going to the telecommunications to put your transmission devices with the military transmitter."

Zevyn checked his watch. It was past midnight. "I will be waiting by the shuttle for your com-link transmission once everything is complete."

Wraith Blade sunk over the armrest of one of the sofas, dangling her legs seductively over the side, smiling at the men's attention as they looked lustfully to her. Wraith Blade unhooks her scabbard of knives and blades, and then slowly zips off her black body suit, revealing a slender, fit body underneath. "I have a meeting with a man called the Technician. He should have the missile downloads for us." She teasingly wiggled an ankle as she anchored an arm over the back of the sofa. She sat with her arms, abdomen, and legs showing. Wraith Blade was left with a burgundy, long sleeve Henley tank top, and spandex pants and mini skirt. "Take Demolisher with you, just in case you run into trouble" said Zevyn.

Demolisher turned from the computer screen and looked to her. "I've already installed the encrypted data for the warheads and downloaded the virus Wraith. We just need the applications installed."

Kelvar, who has been the one mostly in charge of Chaos attacks on the military facilities, slowly glanced to the screen behind Demolisher. He nodded, his ruthless chuckle echoing through the building. "Good. Everything is going as planned. This planet will soon be ours."

CHAPTER TWO

The elegant Chez restaurant was busy with clamorous lively chatter and laughter. The soft lighting amorously set the perfect place for David to undertake the biggest moment of his life. He watched the dim light of the candles dance from the arrangements at other tables, seeing the blissful faces of the couples. Some were romantic, others celebratory, and still others simply content. Tonight, he wanted his and Maria's to be all of those.

David's arm rested on the white tablecloth of the round table. Beside his untouched crème Brule' rum pie his hand was nearly trembling with anticipation. His fingers toyed with the small blue velvet covered jewelry box.

He looked to the doorway, but only the attractive host stood there, looking through the reservations. No Maria.

A shadow fell over his table as he contemplated the jewelry box. Maria was late; she'd called and said she couldn't get there until later, but he still worried his stomach into knots. He looked up to his waitress, Jill, as she glanced over his shoulder.

She gently smiled, seeing his eager face turn to her. "You seem a little edgy today," she noted, smiling wider than her waiting job required. "Not like you to be alone. Anything wrong? You haven't even touched your favorite pie."

He sighed. "Just getting ready to make the most important decision of my life." He debated sharing the moment, but then turned and held the box up to her. A woman's opinion would help at a moment like this. He lifted the spring lid.

Jill's blue eyes widened at the sight of the ring inside. "Oh, my! Congratulations! It's a beautiful ring. Don't worry," she said, giving him a knowing wink. "Maria loves you. Oh, you'll be okay. I know she'll say yes." She glanced to the doorway. "Look, here she comes now."

Maria was standing at the entryway, looking around at the room full of diners. Her gaze rested on David, who was looking her way with a grin spread over his face. Jill discreetly moved off.

David stood up when Maria crossed the room and met him.

"Aye, Dios Mio!" she said jubilantly, planting a kiss on his cheek. "Man, what a day! I just finished my gymnastics and weight training. I'm exhausted."

"Good to see you, Maria," he said, pulling out her chair for her.

She slid into it and smiled as he pushed her to the table. "Ah, so gentlemanly tonight."

"I'm always a gentleman with you," he said, giving her smooth cheek a kiss before resuming his seat. Her face was flushed and bright, lively as always. She was definitely a spark in his world.

"...and I still need more strength," she was saying, sighing for more oxygen. "I have to make the community center tonight. I'll need every bit of energy I can get."

"Make sure you leave some time for me," he said with a devilish grin.

She gave him a flirty smile and a faint blush. "Always."

"I know how you feel. I'm running near empty on the energy stats myself. Boy, this forensic science class is really getting to me, too." He set his hand over the small ring box she hadn't yet spotted.

She leaned over the table and lowered her voice. "My Biology Three class is the same. I have a paper due in a week and I am only halfway through."

David couldn't wait any longer. He took her hand as she made a wave over the unlit candle centerpiece between them. "Maria, do you think you would want to marry me? I mean, I am far from perfect, but I love you with all my heart."

She made only a small gasp, her fingers clasping inside his. She blinked back her surprise and pressed her nose against his. "Hell, yeah... You are the love of my life! David, we have known each other since we were kids. I think I have loved you since third grade," she admitted with a soft giggle. "You know that. Just say the word and I am all yours."

He grinned wider as she leaned farther over the table and kissed him soundly on the lips.

He slid the small box with his other hand so that it was between them and flipped its lid open. Her gaze dropped to the snapping sound, eyes widening. Before she could speak, he took out the one-carat diamond engagement ring. Without releasing her hand, he knelt beside the table and looked up at her.

"You are my best friend," he said earnestly, "my shoulder to lean on and the one person I know I can count on. You're the love of my life. You're my one and only, my everything. I realize it's you that I want to spend the rest of my life with." He took a breath. "So, Ms. Maria Velasquez, will you marry me?"

She gave a little squeal. "Oh, David I cannot believe it. Yes I'll marry you!"

He took the ring and placed it on her slender finger, watching her smile light up even more, making her eyes glimmer, and verging on happy tears.

A sudden eruption of clapping around them made them aware again of the other diners. Every table's occupants were turned to the couple, smiling and with a few whistles as Maria leaned over and pulled David into an embrace. He kissed her deeply, feeling her excitement nearly lunge through her body.

"Cheers!" someone called out.

"Bravo, lad!" an elderly man dining nearby said in a deep French accent.

"You have made me the happiest woman in the world," Maria said, parted from David only a few inches, eyes straying from his face briefly to admire the ring on her hand where her arm was wrapped around his beck. "Oh, David...!"

"I'm still too nervous to eat," he said.

She leaped from her chair, pulling at his hand until he rose to his feet. "I'm too excited for anything! Even dessert!"

He let her tow him out of the restaurant, murmurs of approval still following them from the other diners. Maria passionately kissed David amidst claps and cheers. Life was going to change for both of them.

Unbeknownst to anyone on Earth, a spaceship was nearing the solar system. Amara and Elandrys watched from the viewing window of her private quarters as the stars littered the heavens of space before them. It was a breathtaking view, the points of bright lights twinkling seductively from afar.

But at the moment, the stunningly beautiful and vastness of space was second to the pair standing inside the ship.

Elandrys held the lovely holographic image of Amara as her physical self guided the ship. They were the lone beings in the vessel that was able to self-navigate and maneuver through the star-studded heavens. The backdrop of glittering lights seemed to sparkle just for them, and among that vast darkness was Earth's solar system. Amara's ship systems had already begun scanning the far-off planet.

That planet was not the only thing on Elandrys' mind. Clothed in only black pants as he held Amara's lithe but curvaceous body close to him, he watched the starlight play in her eyes. She was wearing her beige robe that folded in all the right places around her slender shape.

She smiled as he held her in a powerful embrace, and for a moment even her holographic self was able to sense the quickening of the heartbeat in his bare chest against her. She let one hand slide up his muscular arm and around his neck, head tilting back to see his grin. She let her head rest at his chest and looked out the window from her private viewing deck.

"Look, we're approaching another universe," she said, knowing he'd already seen the solar system. Her systems had chimed the arrival moments ago and were already running data-gathering reports.

He sighed, nodding, feeling her smile more against him. "This one seems less radiant," he decided, observing the view with her. "I really appreciated the Raranorian Galaxy's star's incandescent rays."

"I've detected an energy blip on one of my screens," in came the slightly mechanical voice of Amara. "I've noted a life force that appears identical to that of a Sundarian."

Amara shook her head and looked to the nearest voice relay speaker. "This...this can't be!"

"I'm picking up multiple energy life forces that are similar to yours," Amara said to Elandrys.

Amara closed her eyes briefly, nodding, sensing what her ship scanning reports were delivering. She looked up to Elandrys. "Let's take a look." They moved to the closet systems scanning panel. Amara had them located in every chamber, and not a moment went by that she wasn't able to connect with her ship-self. She shook her head as her eyes moved over the panel screen. "It's true."

Elandrys hovered near her shoulder, his gaze on the screen, bewildered. "To my understanding, no Sundarian has been this far away from our galaxy. Is this planet's atmosphere safe for us to enter?"

Amara spoke up: "My systems read yes. That is planet Earth. The Earth's atmosphere has a thin layer of gases that surround it. Earth is composed of nitrogen, oxygen, and argon, carbon dioxide, and trace amounts of other gases. It's breathable for us. It is the third planet from the Sun and the densest and fifth-largest of the eight planets in the solar system. Earth is home to millions of species, including humans."

Amara looked up at him. "It's safe for both of us."

He nodded, watching her eyes take on a more serious depth. "We should look into it."

She nodded and let her systems move the ship towards the new planet. "We're going closer."

Within moments Amara had closed in on planet Earth and entered its gravitational pull. It didn't yield to that pull, not yet, and the two figures in the main viewing room, now fully dressed, watched the blue planet await their decision.

"Amara," Elandrys said seriously concerned, "get us nearer to the planet. Let's see if there is a Sundarian here. And let's see, too, if the Earth people are peaceful or uncivilized."

Amara looked up at him. "Indications show they are a perplexing mix of both. A primitive defense technology, but be careful anyway."

He nodded. "Let's go find out."

Moments later he was in the dispatch chamber, arrayed in the body-hugging black armored suit that felt like second nature to him. It was all Sundarian technology, from the nearly impenetrable gantlet-style gloves to his sleek but thin torso armor. It moved with him, flexibly, allowing full use of every muscle and agility needed for whatever he could possibly face.

Amara is in her more willowy attire. The cape-like cloak fell around her in shades of dove-gray and periwinkle blues with tan lining. Her body was swathed in cobalt and deep lavender leggings and clinging bustier-type corset. The ends of her gray and blue headband swooped down to either side of her face, framing her lovely features falcon-style.

Together they watched as they lowered into the Earth's atmosphere and gradually descend over one of the more populated cities. The fluffy clouds gave way and allowed them a clear look at the alleys and then finally into the industrial part of the metropolis.

Amara opened the entry of at the dispatch room and they both looked to the wristband she wore. A small yellow light on it was blinking. They took their first breaths of the city's dingy air. "That factory there. There's an energy pulse coming from it."

Elandrys looked to the tall, abandoned building two blocks over. He hitched the bag over strap over his shoulder and set his telecom to her channel. "I'm going to take a look. You stay silent to these inhabitants." She approvingly nodded.

Amara lowered the ship more, keeping out of sight of anyone bothering to look up into the night skies. Elandrys quickly made his way through the shadowy streets and cut through a few alleys until he was a couple of buildings from the large abandoned factory. Above him hovered Amara, silent and undetectable.

He warily approached the factory parking lot, watching for any indication of inhabitants. There was none. All that was left of any life were broken pallets, discarded boxes, and junked furniture. He made his way across the broken pavement of the lot and to a side door near the truck loading bay. Inside the building was quiet and dusty, nothing stirring.

He searched it quickly, sharp eyes picking out the minutest movement. A faint reading came from a pile of weapons to one side near what appeared to be a storage room. He went there and nodded, recognizing the heap of items immediately. Weapons.

He angled his wrist to get an image of the weapons. "Look at this," he said into his telecom.

"I see it," Amara said.

He knelt and studied the spent weapons and bands. "These can't be from this planet."

The gloomy interior of the building magnified the dust and musty smell. Most of the dust was undisturbed, except for places where the rats scurried out of sight. Elandrys moved down the wall a few yards and found a stash of pulse guns. He picked a few up, looking at them knowingly. He stuck them in his bag and then turned, hearing something faintly from afar.

"Elandrys," Amara said, "be careful. Some humans are coming towards you. My sensors are reading."

No sooner had she finished speaking than he saw them. From the dim streetlight that seeped in through the painted-over windows, five large forms came up on the other-worlder in black.

All wore cargo pants and one in fatigues. They were decked in leather and chains, armed with assault rifles and wearing black knit hats.

The largest, in cameo fatigues, spoke harshly to Elandrys. "What are you doing here?" he asked in a streetwise slant. "Are you a cop?"

Elandrys kept his guard up. "No."

A thinner thug vociferously chuckled. "I think he's trying to move in on our turf. What's in the bag?"

Something about the men made Elandrys stay on guard. "I don't want your turf. I am not looking for trouble."

The second largest man made a wild pointing gesture. "Well, you just found it. Get him!"

The five swung up their guns, all aimed at Elandrys.

Elandrys shook his head. "I just want to leave."

The fourth thug grinned, showing a mouth of silver. "You'll leave all right," he said in a tinny voice. "In a body bag!"

They all opened fire.

Bullets riddled off the walls as five rifles fired.

Elandrys dodged every bullet. He rushed them during a slight lull in the firing and two men tried to deck him with their rifle stocks. He grabbed the guns and crashed them together, then punched both men. They fell immediately unconscious. A third man grabbed his bag and Elandrys spun, making the man close in enough to intercept a well-placed hit to the stomach.

He scooped up the other guns and energy bands as the remaining two men stepped back in cautionary fear.

"Hey, man, we don't want no trouble," the largest one said, slipping a cartridge into his gun to reload.

Elandrys swung the bag over his shoulder and darted for the door.

"Get him!" one of the men called from behind him as Elandrys made it out the door and slammed it shut behind him.

Elandrys twisted the latch to jam the lock.

The dark night greeted him as the men charged the door, rattling it and swearing. Elandrys looked up as a whooshing breeze drifted over the building. Amara descended swiftly into the parking lot near the trucking door. The ship's door slid open to the dispatch bay and Elandrys stepped in.

Amara greeted him there.

Amara lifted quickly and vacated the parking lot.

Elandrys shrugged off his bag and shook his head. "They're not the brightest of life-forms we've seen."

They promptly start to examine the pulse guns and bands, each recognizing the intelligence that had created the objects.

"This is definitely not from Earth," Elandrys said with terrible concern. He glanced out the small porthole window at the streets as Amara glided away overtop the buildings. "Amara, what is this type of weaponry doing on Earth?"

She was looking at the bands. "That is not Sundarian, but it has the characteristic energy of one." She read the readings her ship's sensors were doing on the new items. "Based on my scans, they are weapons from Toria."

He looked to her quickly. "Toria? The home world of the Toroks?"

"It appears so," she said. "These are versions of the weapons they used to attack Sundaria. They are powered by the Sundarian energy that flows through Sundarian's veins."

He knew it could mean only mean one of two possible things. "Is there a Sundarian here? Or Torok?"

Maria didn't know why she felt like tidying up her messy apartment. It wasn't like her parents were going to drop by unannounced. They were both deep in a cavern's depths in North Africa and weren't due home for at least a day. She knew why the sudden urge to straighten things up; her recent news had made her giddy with excitement and anticipation. She wanted to burn off that energy doing something productive, and her apartment was going to reap the benefits of her recent news.

She giggled as she nodded into the cell phone at her ear, doing a little shimmy dance in her tight t-shirt and shorts as she ran the dust-mop around her small kitchen floor.

"Yes, Camille!" she said into the phone to her best friend. "David and I are engaged! He proposed yesterday."

Camille's voice was laughing in delight, too. "Congratulations, girl. I knew it. I'm so happy for you!"

Maria did a dancing dip with her mop handle. "I have so much planning to do. I have to tell my parents and my brother, Paco. It seems like my whole life is falling into place now."

"You were always waiting for David to ask you. Your parents really like him." Camille sighed joyfully over the phone. "This is going to be such great news for them."

"Yeah, I'm going to my parent's house when they get back tomorrow tonight after I finish my workout at the community center." She stopped and looked around the apartment. She'd put the stacks of folded laundry away later. The floor was clean and she was ready for The Big Call to her parents. As if reading her mind, her phone's call-waiting function blinked. She glanced at the number. "OK, girl, that's Mom calling. I got to go. Take care!"

She pressed the button to hang up with Camille and smiled wider at the name Dr. Anna Velasquez – Mom that was lit on the screen. Both her parents were archaeologists that usually worked together, but she was proud of them, and so always kept their titles with their names Mom and Dad on her phone.

Dr. Anna Velasquez's voice came over the line. "Just calling, checking on you. How is my little girl? "

Maria squealed a little. "Hi, how is it out there? You and Dad having fun on your archaeology research?" She couldn't wait any longer. "I have great news! I'm getting married! Oh, Mom, I am so happy!"

Her mother's immense exhilaration could be heard across the hundreds of miles. "I am so happy for you, too! I can't wait to tell your father. Tell us everything when we get back. I have to go; this call is costing us a fortune and I don't want you to waste your excitement or have the call dropped. I want to hear all about it! Don't forget to check on Paco, too. Te amo."

Maria said exuberantly. "OK, then I will see you when you get back. Te amo también."

In that dark African cave lit only by their field lanterns and headlamps, Doctors Carlos and Anna Velasquez were crowded by centuries of past lives buried deep within the corridors of a former unfamiliar civilization. In Carlos' hands was a small, round, black object, their most recent find. It was as mysterious as Howard Carters' pre-Tutankhamen finds, and neither knew yet whether it was a relic or merely a worthless stone bauble.

Carlos Velasquez adjusted his glasses, eyeing the artifact. "Was that our little girl you were just talking to?" He cleared hit throat in the dank air. "I'm surprised you got any reception down here. How is she doing? Why didn't you put me on?"

Anna smiled widely in the light of their helmet lamps. "You're a busy archaeologist; you're going to be able to talk to her all you want when we get back tomorrow. By the way, she's getting married."

Carlos nearly dropped the round artifact. "What? Our little girl? I can't wait to get back, Dr. Velasquez! A wedding. I am so excited!"

Anna gave a hearty giggle. She nodded and peered more closely at the object he held. "This is the oddest piece." She held a magnifying glass over the side of it, slowly nodding. "I haven't seen anything like this on any of our charts. I don't think it's been mentioned in any catalogs. I can't even tell what time period this is from." She turned his hand over to see the other side of the item. "I need to get this home to study in-depth."

He nodded. "It looks to be some kind of crest representing the sun." He thumb gently pressed over a line of the engraving on one side. "Look at these paintings on the wall." He turned and let his headlamp illuminate the stone wall behind them. They were similar to the object's markings. "Very interesting..."

She gradually moved closer, frowning as she tried to determine the origin of language. "What does this symbol mean?" She pointed to one line engraved in the wall and then looked down the object he held. "I am so anxious to study this in more detail."

He gently blew on a section of the wall etching, nodding slowly. "This looks to be millions or billions of years old." He gestured at the other parts of the wall. All the line etchings showed various scenes with only the two figures. Only two people in these drawings and it look like the same two." He nodded to the other drawings with figures. They were clearly the same two figures depicted in each scene. "This man and woman."

She was looking at another drawing that showed only one human figure. "I see. You're right. Look at this wall, Carlos. There are drawings of only one figure, a woman."

He stepped back and nodded, looking around at the walls lined with different scenes. There was no writing and the only item they'd found was the one he held. It had been placed beneath a small rounded inlet into the wall, like a canonic jar or something to hold necessary items for the afterlife.

"Everything in the cave is a total mystery," he said in awe. "We must get more archeologists back here for a more thorough study." An air of mystery and profound wonder lent his voice. "What have we found down here?"

CHAPTER THREE

The late afternoon in the woods, it is peaceful and still as Elandrys and Amara walked through the trees and foliage. All around them the beauty of Earth was alive with smells and sounds. The birds in the trees and small creatures scurrying in the undergrowth watched the two foreigners with curious eyes.

Elandrys nodded ahead. "This is it."

Amara looked to where he indicated.

The thick trees of the woods were broken by a clearing of snapped tree trunks and scraped vegetation. It wasn't a new crash site, nor was whatever had crashed still there. The circular spot showed some new growth on the broken tree trunks and the new grass had covered some of the ground, but it was still evident that something large had scraped in and plowed straight along the terrain.

Elandrys and Amara closed in on the site, using sharp eyesight looking for the telltale markings of what they suspected. Sure enough, debris that could only have come from a Torok ship was in the brush, broken and useless, but still identifiable.

Amara engaged the settings on her scanner and swept the area.

"This is a Torok shuttle ship debris," Elandrys said knowingly as he bent to pick up a piece of hull. He turned it over, nodding. "The ship doesn't look like it crashed, even though there are broken branches." His gaze rose to the trees, estimating the new growth on the limbs. "It just looks like they had a rough landing."

Amara stood beside him, eyes on the scanner's screen. "There were Sundarians here also." She glanced around, attention settling on a fragment of color on a bush. She went there and picked it up. It was a small torn piece of fabric. "Look," she said as he stood up. "Pieces of Sundarian clothing and discarded energy bands."

She found a few more on the bush and gathered them. "Scanning with my thermo-molecular sensors, these energy bands, this is what I was reading. This is my original location." She rubbed the material between her fingers; it was definitely made from textiles not from Earth. "If the Toroks are here, the question still remains, what part does the Sundarian play on this planet?"

He was pushing the tall grass with one boot, reading the faint prints in the dark dirt. "There are multiple footprints." He looked around to where they led. "Many were here. It doesn't look like there was a battle here, however."

She looked to the sky wistfully. "If we had intergalactic capabilities, I would send a transmission back to Sundaria, to see if there are people still missing in Sundaria." She glanced back to him. "Even if I did, it would take too long for the information to get back to us."

He nodded, giving the area another inspection. "The war has been long over. They would have been found or presumed dead."

They heard the footsteps of a animal moving cautiously among the thick brush in the trees at the perimeter of the site. Something moved again, halting footsteps of something watching them.

Amara took a deep breath of the forest air. She smiled, eyes going to the trees and their unseen observer. "This planet is beautiful," she said with a sigh. "The air, the mountains, the flowers, and trees." She looked behind the way they'd come where the tips of the nearby mountains could be seen over the evergreens. "They have many animals here, too. They are watching us in the shadows. I can sense it."

They both looked to the edge of the trees where the slow footsteps stopped. Elandrys saw Amara glance compassionately to the watcher, and a few moments later, a deer stepped from the trees.

Amara smiled at the deer and beckoned it to come closer. She stretched out her hand and wiggled her fingers, speaking softly.

The deer's large ears pricked forward and it took a few more steps, nose quivering as it tested the air for smells. Amara continued to speak lowly and the animal stepped closer, eventually close enough to sniff her fingers. With slow movements, Amara pet the deer's nose and then moved up to its neck. Elandrys looked on as another deer showed up, curious and debating moving closer.

Suddenly a shot rang out. The deer at Amara's hand bolted away and all the watching deer turned to run.

Amara spun around at the noise of the gunshot, eyes searching the trees. "Humans are near!"

Before Elandrys could speak, another voice drifted through the woods.

"Come on!" a man called. "They went this way!"

More gunshots rang out through the trees. The sounds of the deer charging away faded.

Two hunters wearing camouflaged hunting clothing and safety orange hunting caps ran out from the trees, shotguns in their hands. They stopped when they saw the oddly-dressed foreigners.

"Stop!" Amara cried at them, raising a hand palm-side out. "Don't! You are going to kill them!"

Before either hunter could react, she ran to one and grabbed his gun, angling it away from the way the deer had run.

Not to be denied their sport, the man shoved Amara away, trying to retain his gun. The other man grabbed her arm and pushed her aside.

"What do you think you're doing out here?" he demanded. "This is deer season!"

The first man was watching Elandrys as he stepped closer. "Yeah, so you two can beat it!"

"But they're innocent animals," Amara said.

The first grabbed her by the cape clasp at her throat and shook her, nearly choking her. "We're hunting here, sweetheart, not running a PETA refuge!"

Elandrys snatched the man's hunting vest back and smashed a fist into his face. The hunter dropped his gun and grabbed his bleeding mouth. He fell to his back and scooted away from the Sundarian.

The second hunter tried to intervene but Elandrys kicked the gun from his hands. It went twirling away into a tree trunk, smacking with such force that the barrel bent.

Elandrys grabbed the man on the ground by his collar and heaved him to his feet. "Have you seen any other people in the area or did you shoot them, too?"

The hunter shook his head, eyes wide and frightened, his bleeding mouth forgotten. "N-No, we haven't seen anybody. We are just hunting deer. We don't shoot people."

The second hunter nodded numbly, glancing from his damaged gun at the tree base to Elandrys. "Not people. Never people, man."

Elandrys looked between the men for a moment, studying their terrified and seemingly earnest expressions. He turned to Amara and nodded. "They cannot help us."

She gave each man a disappointed look, and then stepped back.

Before the men's very eyes, she stretched her arms high over her head, as if reaching for the stars. Her long hair tumbled down her back and her cape swirled around her in dusky tan and blues. She swiftly lowered her arms into an inverted V and then transformed into the sleek spaceship.

The hunters fell back at the spectacle as she lifted into the air, sweeping Elandrys inside the ship as Amara ascended atop the trees.

The leaves and grass swayed and rustled as the ship departed in a whoosh.

The hunters stood dumbfounded, gawking up at the ship that zipped out of sight over the trees, heading for the city.

The first hunter swallowed with disbelief. "Man, I'm not going to say anything if you don't say anything..."

The second hunter was equally amazed as they were left looking into the void of the late afternoon sky. It was incredible.

He finally found his voice. "I'm sure I won't."

The Velasquez family home was quiet as Maria opened the front door. She looked around for her parents, but heard nothing. Usually when they were home, and there was music – either slow jazz or her mother's Big Band era swing – playing throughout the house.

Maria set her keys on the entryway table as she looked into the living room. "Hola, Mom, Dad!" she called.

There was no return greeting.

She set her bag down by the edge of the wall to the living room and looked around. All the overstuffed brown furniture was empty, neat, and even the sound system was silent, just as they'd left it before going to Africa.

She stepped to the kitchen beyond the living room. The counters were clean and tidy, the stove empty of cooking accessories. She frowned, wishing to smell the delicious aroma of her mother's special Cajun gumbo. "Where are you?" She glanced to the telephone on the stand near the dining room table that opened to the living room. "Are you home?"

She went into the dining room off the modest kitchen and checked the messages. One. She pressed the button.

"...back soon, Maria," came her mother's voice, sounding very far away. "...to our chins in the lab at the museum," she said through the static on the line. "...bad reception because we're in the museum's data vault. That's part of what we found on the table... don't you?"

Maria looked to the small, round black object on the dining room table. "I guess that's you, huh?"

She went to the table and took a closer look at the black stone amulet. A very big amulet, she thought, weighing it in her hand. She set it back down; her parents' fascination with the past wasn't as ingrained in her. "Oh, I'm so exhausted," she said to no one, sighing and rubbing one shoulder. "And I need more work on the floor. My limberness is suffering."

It was an exaggeration; Maria's agility was fine, but she wanted to excel. She wanted to spend every waking moment at the community center, but now with a wedding in her future – now she had other priorities, too.

She glanced back to the black amulet and picked it up, studying it better this time in the late day's light through the windows. It was truly stunning, she had to admit. It was smooth and round and in the center it had an indistinct shape, with a beautiful design on the front. She wondered if it was Egyptian or Sumerian, or even older. She smiled. "You are rather lovely," she told it, smiling wider, feeling an indescribable draw to the object, to hold it, to understand it. "Kind of silly to think something like this has any personality, but it is beautiful. One of the treasures they brought back from Africa, I guess. They're at the museum, so I guess it's me and you, Arty-fact."

She set the object back on the table and went into the living room. "Oh, too tired to eat," she said with a yawn, slumping onto the sofa.

She found the remote control for the TV on the coffee table and aimed it at the large screen set across the room. She found a decent station and felt sleep tempt her. She had been working hard at the center, and she was improving. She pulled off her over-shirt and yoga pants and sat in her tank top and panties, watching some documentary on endangered species.

Within moments, however, she was slumped over on the decorative pillows to her left side, sleeping, her workout having taken its toll.

As she slept, the black artifact on the table behind her in the dining room began to glow, seeming to absorb the setting sun's rays within its dark interior. The rays of sun passed into and through the black artifact until it was charged and glowing with energy. The illumination rested on Maria, bathing her in its strong glow, empowering her, transforming her.

Maria slept on, unaware.

The artifact quietly relayed its power from centuries and time, endowing the young woman.

The phone rang shrilly.

Maria startled awake. She ran a hand through her hair, and then frowned at the way her body looked. She sat up more and the object's light washed over her.

She ran a hand over her thigh, feeling nothing different, just the strange light, wondering. She looked over the back of the sofa at the dining room table.

There the amulet seemed to glow in the setting sun's final rays.

Is that amulet shedding its light on me? she wondered.

"...still at the museum and have a meeting until late tonight," her mother was saying over the answering machine. "We'll see you soon, sweetheart."

There was a click of the line hanging up, but Maria was engrossed with the light playing over her body. She looked from the object to the sun she could see through the dining room windows.

That's what it is, she told herself.

Still exhausted, she lay back down, unaware.

Maria slept well that night and awoke with an extraordinary feeling of rejuvenation. She was still on the sofa, thoughts of her parents and David on her mind. She stretched her arms overhead, opening her eyes slowly.

And then she opened them more quickly.

Her arms felt different, more powerful, and stronger.

She frowned at them; they even looked a little different. The regular muscles along her forearms were more defined, and her upper arms felt tighter.

"What's going on?" she asked, sitting up completely. The movement was swifter than she expected and she realized that her abdominal muscles were tighter, too. She pulled up her tank top.

To her bewilderment, a row of abdominal muscles encased her stomach where before it had been flat but not too cut. She ran a hand down her stomach, smiling at the muscular feel. It wasn't ripped like the bodybuilding women she'd seen, but defined and smooth, shapely for a woman's body.

"Wow, I guess all those crunches paid off," she said, giggling. "Kind of some latent development."

She stood up and looked at her legs. Her movements felt more graceful, stronger, and steadier. She ran a hand down her thigh, amazed. She'd always been fit, but now the bit of excess fatty tissue covering her muscles was thinner. Still, she determined, angling her head over her back to see a well-developed calf muscle, not too cut – not like those skeletal bodybuilding women – but real muscle making real, natural curves.

And, she felt stronger. Immensely stronger.

"Oh, my..." she said, smiling more. "I'll bet I could fly if I jumped high enough."

49

It was just a joke, but when she glanced around the room, her gaze fell on the amulet on the table. In her dreams she thought she saw it glowing, an illumination that covered her and seemed to encase her in light.

She shook her head. "Juice first," she decided.

She went into the kitchen and opened the refrigerator door. To her surprise, she wrenched the entire door off the hinges. Out tumbled several items from the door and bottom shelf.

"Oh, no!" She leaned the door to the counter, aghast at it – and what would her parents think? -- and knelt to pick up the items that had fallen out. "Oh, boy, I'm going to hear about this..."

She put the bottles and containers back inside the refrigerator and spend a moment trying to lean the door back into place. It set against the refrigerator opening, but still wasn't a good seal.

"Maybe I'll see if David can help me with that," she said as she headed to the dining room again, her eyes on the amulet. "This is too odd."

She glanced at the full length mirror at the hallway. She was indeed more muscular. She stopped and turned this way and that, shocked at the change in her body.

"What has happened?" she murmured.

She went to the table and picked up the amulet. It was dark now, all black, with no glow.

She nodded slowly. "I feel strangely stronger." She turned the amulet, seeing nothing different about it. Nothing is different in the house but me and this, she thought. "This somehow has changed me. I need to find out exactly what this is that Mom and Dad brought from Africa."

She set the object in her bag and went to take a shower.

That night after her college classes, Maria stopped by the community center as usual for her workout. She'd packed the black artifact in her bag to study more, but promised herself she'd take good care of it, and return it by the time her parents got home.

She went through her normal routine of gymnastic warm-up and stretches. Everything seemed to move easier, and she couldn't help but marvel at her new dexterity. She finished a complicated floor routine of general leaps and exercises, and then glanced to herself in the wall-length mirror that ran one complete side of the gym floor.

Maria glanced to the balance beam; she made a perfect somersault onto and off the beams. "I think my work is paying off!"

"Hey, girl! Looking good!" a young woman called to her across the tumbling bodies.

Maria glanced to the balance beam where the assistant coach for the intramural gymnastics team was letting her team take a breather. She flashed Maria a thumbs-up.

Maria smiled and returned the gesture. "Thanks!"

"Yeah, you're looking real strong there," called a guy Maria knew as Matt. He was at the elevated rings in the next section of gym. He gave her a quick bow and a wink.

She smiled and waved a hand back. "I think my work is paying off!"

Matt chuckled in agreement and turned back for his turn on the rings.

She took a deep breath, smiling at her image in the mirror. So it wasn't just her noticing it; she was different. And, she knew it had something to do with that strange artifact her parents had brought back.

She turned back to the floor mat, stretching her arms overhead. She wondered just how much better she was.

She took a running start and planted a springing handstand into a double flip into a giant vertical leap. She landed solidly on both feet, sticking the landing. Usually that combination – if she got through that first double flip – toppled her off the mat. She was barely breathing hard.

She felt stronger than ever.

Around her the appreciative glances looked her way, a few murmurs of awe and a couple of clappings from the intramural team members. Most were junior high girls, and Maria gave them a big smile and a wave.

She still wondered just how much better she was; how high could she jump? How much more limber was she?

"Heads up!" a man called.

Maria pivoted at the voice and without thinking, reached a hand up and snatched the flying object zooming toward her head. She caught it with ease.

She opened her hand to see a discus.

"Wow! You really caught that?" someone called out.

"Did you see that? Unbelievable!" another person shouted.

Around her the other people in the gymnasium were stunned at Maria's reflexes.

"Hey!" Matt called to the mesh fenced discus practice area far across the gym. "What happened? You could have hurt someone!"

Two young men at the discus area were walking to the outside of the mesh netting where a large hole was visible.

"There's a rip in the fencing," one said, trying to flip up the flap of torn mesh. "Sorry!"

Maria looked at the hard rubber discus in her hand and then back to the two men.

"You really caught that?" one said, shaking his head. "You've got some eye, girl! Becker throws at eighty miles an hour!"

Maria spends hours in the gym finding out just how much she has changed. She was astonished at herself. The other man, Becker, looked humbly at Maria. "Hey, yeah... Nice catch. I'm glad no one got hurt."

Maria flipped the discus into the air and then flung it back at the two men. It cut cleanly through the air, spinning.

Neither man caught it, ducking to let the spinning discuss whiz by. It broke through the netting like tissue paper.

Whistles of astonishment went through the air.

Maria giggled a little. "Sorry!" she called to Becker and his friend as they glanced to her with amazement. "I've never thrown one of those before!"

Becker shook his head. "Had to be a hundred miles an hour! That's some arm, girl!"

It was true, Maria thought. It was real. Something had changed her into a new woman.She liked what she saw.

CHAPTER FOUR

That night a new person stood atop the twelve-story buildings overlooking the bustling city streets and parks. She was slender and strong, her body swathed in black and blue Lycra, her face hidden by a mask. Her dark hair was pulled up into a high ponytail at the back of her head above her blue head wrap.

Maria wanted to use her newfound abilities. She stood looking down on that city, smiling at the feel of her new vigorous body.

Maria had changed into some of the clothes she had in her locker at the community center. She'd made use of the deep blue leotard and leggings she'd worn for dance practice, and a piece of thin black cloth for her mask, she was ready.

Ready for what? Maria thought, she wasn't quite sure.

She spotted a few cars in the parking lot of the park, and then with easy agility, leaped down to the street below her four-story high perch. She landed gracefully and raced to the parking lot.

She was there in no time. She felt more alive than ever, stronger, fleeter, as if she could pull down the very moon if she had a lasso. She walked over to one of the cars, a small coupe, and gave it a brief study.

Could it be possible? she wondered.

"Let's find out," she told herself.

She went to the front of the car and looked to the windshield. No one inside. She crouched and hooked her hands palm-up under the front bumper. She slowly rose up, lifting as she'd seen Olympic athlete lift, and heaved the car from its tires.

She grinned, gritting her teeth as she straightened, and then stood upright. The car was off its front tires, at her mercy

She laughed and slowly set it back down.

She looked around, spying a few other cars and a large SUV.

She lifted them all. One by one, Maria lifted the Mustang, the Buick, the Ford F150 truck, and then the Escalade.

Each was at her mercy. She stood with her hands on her hips, breathing only slightly harder. She was indeed strong.

"Now for speed," she said thoughtfully, glancing around at the still cars. "Something...fast..."

A train whistle blew in the distance.

"That's it!" she cried.

Over the next hour, Maria raced every train she could find – and won – and lifted increasingly heavier vehicles. Rather than growing tired after each accomplishment, she grew stronger-feeling, ready for any new challenge.

When she was out of new things to outrun or lift, she sprinted to a six—story building that overlooked one of the poorer sections of the city. Against the pale moon that stretched across the horizon, she watched the grimy streets below. By the light of night she'd found herself anew. The darkness had given birth to a new life. She could feel it in her bones.

I feel the night's beauty inside my soul, she thought, taking in the city by night. It comforts me like an acquaintance long forgotten. She closed her eyes as the breeze ruffled her ponytail and head rag ties. Oh, night, calm and intoxicating, she thought, inhaling the air, I embrace your tender touch.

She opened her eyes and was still caught up in that thought as she saw three men with ski masks over their heads dash into a corner store at the street.

"Here's my chance to see what I can do," she told herself.

She leapt down from the rooftop, landing directly before the three robbers as the darted from the store. The men stopped short as she blocked them.

She looked at the men, who all had a bag of stolen goods in their hands. "Maybe you want to pay for that?"

The largest grinned beneath his mask. "Well, maybe you want to try and make us."

Maria lifted an eyebrow. "You can do this the easy way, the right way, or you can test my mood."

One of the other two men chuckled. "And what's your mood, honey?"

The third man set his bag down and balled his hands into fists. He took a step toward her. "So you wanna play rough, hey, girlie?"

Maria bolted for him. Lightning fast, she karate-chopped a hand to the back of his head and spun around, kicking him in his pudgy belly. He landed on his back, gasping for air.

The second man rushed her, but she pivoted and planted a heel to his throat, knocking him against the store's brick wall. She spun around and double kicked the first man, driving him into a street-light post.

She turned to look at the other two men; they lay slumped on the sidewalk, drifting into dazed confusion. She glanced to the man at the streetlight. He was also unconscious.

The store owner peeked meekly out of the store door. He gawked at the men lying around, and then looked to Maria. "Oh, thank you so much!"

She smiled at him, bushing her ponytail over her shoulder. "You're welcome." She gave the robbers a disdainful look. "Make sure you call the police. Have a nice night."

She leaped to the top of his store, and then raced off into the night.

Something about helping the store owner made Maria wants to do more, help more, give back. She continued on through the city that night, wandering from top to top of the buildings of Lexington Park city. Everywhere shadows lurked, hiding a multitude of possible misdeeds. The city needed her, needed someone to right wrongs.

She'd never seen the city this way, all the streets and alleys. It looked like a maze, able to hide nearly anything.

Yet, she saw the good and the bad, and in ways she had never seen before, in ways that she had ignored as her former weaker self.

She stood atop a roof and looked down at it all. "This is incredible," she breathed, feeling rejuvenated. "Incredible and awesome. I truly can use my new abilities to help like never before. I think I'll call myself Onyx, after the black color of the amulet, which somehow transformed me. Maria now Onyx, looks over the dazzling city skyline.

Across Lexington Park city at one of the apartment buildings in the Westside, the seedier side of life had met up in a very contemporary apartment. The semi-plush interior of the main living area was lined with top tier computer equipment and monitors that showed the hallways of the building, exteriors and alleys, and a few others that were running programs and cracking high profile codes.

Three enormous guards stood at the door, watching the occupants.

In the center of the living room before a table, was the master of the computer-hacker domain, a tall, lanky man named simply Andy. His long brown hair was tied back in a braid as he leaned over the coffee table before him, deftly fixing together the components of a slim motherboard. As if the armed guards at the door weren't enough, beside him leaning against the back of the couch was his girlfriend, a rifle leaned to her shoulder.

She fondly toyed with the gun's barrel, cat-like green eyes on Wraith Blade and Demolisher standing across the coffee table. Wraith Blade held a briefcase. There was no love lost in her gaze on the woman. Andy grunted something at her, but his girlfriend pretended not to hear.

Andy sat back from the table, giving the completed motherboard a quick grin as if he'd just solved a Rubric's Cube rather than mastered the circuitry. He eyed the stack of computer discs beside the board and then looked up at Demolisher and Wraith Blade.

"All right, I can talk to you now." He nudged his girlfriend with a pointy elbow to break her stare on Wraith Blade. "Now that the worms are installed in the main frame," he said, nodding to one of the computers running a program at the wall counter, "you can now override the encrypted pass codes and reset the launch sequences. The program is still vulnerable to the security virus protocols of the system. If they are recognized, they can still be reset back within sixteen seconds. The phase three logarithms are not known too many people," he added with no real concern, "so they probably will not be attentive of it; but if they do, it cannot be traced back to it origin point."

Demolisher nodded. "Once we download the disc, we will have total control?"

Andy nodded smugly. "Yes, that's correct. This is for you." He leaned forward again and rifled through the stack of computer discs beside the motherboard.

Wraith Blade set the briefcase full of money on the table.

Andy grinned and handed her one of the computer discs.

She looked at it, knowing the control it would give them.

"Thank you," Demolisher said. "And this is for you – an early retirement." In one smooth move, he grabbed Andy's shirt and pulled him nearly across the table. He punched him in the face, cracking bone.

Andy stumbled back, wiping his tender jaw as his girlfriend scooted away from him. She nervously clutched the rifle.

"This is what you do?" Andy said, somewhat thickly with his jaw now sore. "You try to double-cross me? You will never get away with it. Get them!"

The armed guards and Andy's girlfriend went into action, opening gunfire on Wraith Blade and Demolisher.

Wraith Blade pulled two blades and lunged for Andy, ducking the bullets. His girlfriend recoiled, her gun firing at the door near the guards. Wraith Blade yanked Andy to the computer counter and stabbed his hand to the wall.

He screamed in pain.

"Don't move!" she ordered.

Street-side from the lush apartment, those gunshots rang out loud. In the Jeep parked beside the curb, David Ramirez and GSA Agent Marcelle both looked to the building.

"Gun shots," David said, throwing open the Jeep door. "This could be our chance to stop them!"

He dashed out of the Jeep.

Marcelle tried to reach for him, but David was already on the sidewalk. "No, we need are just here for surveillance, David!"

David paused, looking from the apartment building stairs back to Marcelle. "Why? It's just two of them. We can take them. Come on."

Marcelle shook his head as David sprinted for the building's double doors. "David, no! David, come back! Are you crazy?"

Inside the building, David ran up the staircase, following the gunshots that were now more sporadic, as if the shooters were actually aiming. Agent Marcelle was close behind now, following him with his gun drawn. They reached the third floor where the noise was loudest and went down the hallway. It was empty.

They found the room with the most noise, sounding like a battle was being waged inside.

Without waiting for Marcelle's word, David kicked the door in.

The door broke open and the scene inside wasn't what either David or Marcelle expected.

A tall man stood to one wall, his hand painfully stabbed to it, oozing blood down his arm. The bodyguards were hiding behind the blocked furniture, shooting opportunistically at Demolisher. A girl's head could be seen poking up from behind the sofa, the barrel of a rifle beside her upset hair.

There were also two other figures.

David took a ready stance, gun outstretched before him. "FBI! Everyone put your weapons down!"

Marcelle followed David into the apartment, but to him, there were fewer people in the room. His stare locked on Wraith Blade, memories of her flooding him.

Wraith Blade had noticed him, too. "You? Here?" Disbelief was in her tone.

He shook his head at her. "Stop. You don't have to be a part of this."

The gunfire stopped, mostly from confusion from the scene between the two.

Wraith Blade gave Marcelle a sad but flirty smile. "What? You think you can stop us?"

Marcelle didn't let their past fumble him. "I know I can!"

Demolisher was busy fighting the guards, and still looking for Wraith Blade. His eyes found her. Demolisher looked between the two, sensing something more at play. "Wraith Blade, let's move! Hurry!"

His order seemed to break the lull in gunfire and the guards fired again, this time at David and Demolisher. David returned fire.

With a mighty roar, Demolisher charged the guards en masse.

Marcelle leaped over the sofa as Wraith Blade tried to elude the ensuing riot. He grabbed her wrist but she wielded a slashing blade at him.

He released her wrist and leaped back.

"This doesn't concern you!" she said. She didn't have to miss; her blades were true.

His face softened some. "...I can help you."

She returned a chilled smile. "Help me? I loved you and you left me. Is that what people in love do?"

There was a loud grunt of pain and Marcelle saw Andy sag at the wall a little as his girlfriend pulled the knife from his hand. Andy muted his curses, cradling his bloody hand to his stomach.

Marcelle shook his head at Wraith Blade. "No. I left because I had too. I left the life you wanted to live. I never stopped loving you."

She took a deep breath. "You know I had no choice."

His voice lowered. "You could've come with me."

From across the room, Demolisher was conscious to their reunion. "Hurry, Wraith! Program the warheads! I will take care of these guys!" He saw the enraptured look in her eyes as she spoke with the agent. "Wraith, move!"

She jolted from her past and slipped past Marcelle. She went to the computer running the ballistics program and began the arming sequence.

Demolisher punched the enormous guards to the floor with a heavy blow, but they scurried away.

"Come on!" one of them yelled to Andy's girlfriend.

She abandoned Andy, who was leaned to a wall as he held his bloody hand, and exited the room with the guards.

Wraith Blade avoided Marcelle as he made a grab for her, her eyes intent on finishing the arming sequence.

"Here!" David called from the hallway. "I got one!"

Andy had slipped out of the room.

Torn between his past and present, Marcelle followed David's voice to the hallway.

Demolisher leaned over Wraith Blade, the stray bullets bouncing off of his body as she finished the sequence. "Ready?"

"We're good."

They took a few moments to place several explosives around the apartment.

Demolisher and Wraith Blade go the roof and leaps to the adjoining building. Demolisher and Wraith Blade stood on a nearby building, watching the window to the doomed apartment Andy had used. In the street below, Andy was being apprehended by the agents.

"Too close" said Demolisher as both Demolisher and Wraith Blade raced away.

"What happened back there?" he called as they leaped to the next rooftop. "You know; with that cop."

She didn't look to him, landing on the next roof and running on. "He was someone I knew back in China. Someone I once cared for; even loved."

He steeled any emotional response. "He is going to be a problem for us. He knows too much about our operation."

Her voice was level when she spoke. "Leave him to me, Demolisher. I will take care of him myself. You don't have to worry about him."

He stopped on the next rooftop. "How do I—?"

She turned to face him and said sharply, "Because I said so."

He knew there was more to her story but didn't ask. "Let's go."

Neither knew that far below that building, on the street stood Marcelle, looking up at the last glimpse he had of his past love. He watched, breathless from chasing after the pair, hoping to catch another sight of her.

As if sensing him, Wraith Blade peeked over the edge of the rooftop. She was without the man known as Demolisher, but Marcelle knew it was Wraith Blade – his Angela – and he remembered every wave of her hair, every curve of her body. She looked at Marcelle, wanting to hold him; instead turned and ran out of sight.

Marcelle sighed and headed back to the apartment. He could see the police cars already parked at the building.

By the time he got to the apartment, the rooms were crawling with police, some hauling out large crates of weapons from other rooms. David was showing them around, reliving the shootout. Seeing David made Marcelle's irritation reignite.

"What the hell was that?" he demanded of him. "You could have just blown this whole operation. You put my life and yours in danger."

David gestured to the computers and caches of weapons the police had found in the other rooms. "Look what we got. Stolen computers, all these weapons."

Marcelle waved it off. "We don't have anything. We still don't know what they were doing here. You were just supposed to do forensics, nothing more."

David looked guilty, but frowned at him. "How does Wraith Blade know you?" He raised an eyebrow. "How come you never told me this information?"

Marcelle shared some of that guilt on David's face. "That doesn't matter now. They got away. They've seen us and now they are on to us. Our cover is gone." He let accusation seep into his tone. "What do we do now? They could go into hiding."

He brushed past David and stormed out of the apartment. The officers watched him go.

David sighed, disappointed in himself. "I just wanted to get this over with so I can get married."

An officer that was bent over to inspect one of the computer electrical cords stood up and gravely looked to them all. "There are explosives here. I think we should all get out quickly and call in the Bomb Squad to handle this."

David groaned.

Another officer nodded. "Let's go. I'll make the call."

As the last of the police officers were coming out of the apartment, the bombs exploded with a fiery blasted that brightened the night with a burst of orange-red color. Because of the power of the blast, the last men that were exiting the building were thrown into the cars and the street concrete pavement.

Dense, black smoke was now saturating the air. Everyone escaped the explosion, but many were slightly burned and injured from glass and flying debris.

"Is everyone alright?" Marcelle yelled out.

Marcelle looked at the police officers, checking them, making sure they were not badly injured. He slowly started to get positive answers from the police officers lying on the ground.

Flames now raged from the building. The coughing police officers began to gather their wits again, they looked at the damaged building and blazing fire, they were glad to be alive.

Marcelle finally turn looking at the building, "If there was any evidence in that building we could have used, it's all gone now, they made sure of that" Marcelle said irately.

Across the city, Maria had finished her first pass through the streets and rooftops. She was still so thrilled at the venture, feeling every bit as powerful and confident.

She stood in her apartment, looking at herself in the large mirror in the living room. She was only in her underclothes, and with her new, more muscular body, she was tempted to strike a bodybuilding pose.

But she didn't.

"I don't know much about what you are," she said, addressing the black artifact still in her bag near the table, "but you have changed my body to this."

She flexed a few bicep poses, and then turned and looked at her thighs in the mirror. Nice and tight, she thought. She jumped in place and then did a few precise somersaults in the large living room.

She literally sprang to her feet. "Any other time I would just about kill myself trying to do that," she said to her image in the mirror. "Now I can do this perfectly. This is sure going to help me in gymnastics. I'm going to try out for the state team. I know I can make it to the finals, maybe even take first place." She smiled wider. "Maybe track, too. I'll go all-state."

She looked to the stack of clothing she had on the sofa. Some were a bit loose-fitting before, but now with her new body, she knew they would fit, and look good on her.

"What am I supposed to do?" she said, pulling on a vibrant purple skirt. It slid right on, snapping easily at her waist. "Should I tell David, Camille? My Mom and Dad?"

She found a deep blue halter top and tied it on, admiring the look in the mirror.

"I'll tell David first. Somehow I trust him the most. Mom and Dad would worry themselves to death. 'What did we do to our little girl?'" She giggled a little. "I can hear them saying it now. Mom crying out loud like it's the end of the world. No... I'll tell only David and then take it from there." She sighed and looked to the clothing awaiting her. "I know he would only think what's best for me. I guess that's why I love him so much."

She took out a dark purple shirt and a pair of dark purple tights – she loved the color – and put them on and looked at herself in the mirror. She pulled her long wavy hair back away from her face and tied it up. She reached for her mask that lay on the sofa. She had designed it quickly, but still liked how it looked. She put it on, turning her head different ways in the mirror. On impulse, she took off her shirt and the tights and found her new persona's outfit: the deep blue shirt, leotard and leggings.

She put them on and stood before the mirror. The mask was shaped like two black diamonds that framed her dark eyes, giving her an intense look. She nodded at herself.

"I like this. Until I find out more about this artifact," she told her reflection, "it'll remain a mystery to me."

She looked at the accessories on the sofa, among them a few belts and gloves.

"With a few adjustments," she said, picking up a gold belt made of graduated ovals that fit her slender waist nicely, "I'll be ready to take on anything in the city."

She looked at herself again in the mirror, liking how the golden belt added to her attire. "...Yes. I am now

Onyx."

CHAPTER FIVE

Police lights flashed across the café's windows as officers surrounded the newly demolished luxury apartment building. The downtown of Lexington Park City was awash in red and blue as onlookers watched the Bomb Squad tape off the area, ordering people to back up and disperse. Most just watched, enthralled.

Daniel and Stanley joined Angela in the nearby café. Demolisher had left to bring the disc to the Toroks waiting at the warehouse.

After breakfast, leaving that café and now concealed in regular street clothes were Polar – now dressed simply as Stanley – Mystic-as Daniel, and Wraith Blade-as Angela. Anyone in the crowd would have seen them as Stanley, Daniel, and Angela. No one even looked their way.

The three watched the effects of their handiwork, recognizing David Ramirez on the scene talking with the police officers. Without a word to each other, Stanley, Daniel, and Angela gradually joined the crowd of onlookers.

Angela nodded to where David was speaking with the Bomb Squad chief. "It's the cop from the other day. From the jewelry heist."

Daniel looked to where she indicated. "Sure is. All right, blend in carefully," he said in a low tone. "Let's get closer to hear what's going on. After that we'll follow him to see where he goes."

Stanley and Angela nodded and they dispersed into the crowd of people. It was easy to lose themselves in the mass and to keep their faces hidden from the surveillance cameras and any nosey officers. For a few moments they wandered among the onlookers, watching and wary. After a long moment Stanley met up with Daniel.

"They have said things about us," he said.

Daniel nodded. "Do they have any evidence on us?" he asked as Angela joined them.

"I don't know," she said, hearing the question.

They watched the Bomb Squad carefully enter what was left of the building. A moment later David Ramirez headed for a car parked with the squad cruisers.

"We have to make sure all evidence of our presence is destroyed" says Mystic. "I don't want anything leading them to us or to the presence of the Toroks."

Stanley's gaze followed the FBI agent. "Let's go."

Agent Marcelle and David were unaware of the three super-powered beings following them from the devastated apartment building. They drove a few blocks and headed into the more residential part of the city and turned onto a street that few people were aware of.

It was a single-story house with a modest yard, perfect disguise for a FBI safe house. They parked at the carport where two other cars already were and went inside the back door of the house.

What they didn't see was Mystic, Wraith Blade, and Polar alight to a nearby three-story rooftop that overlooked the safe house. They touched down and crouched, watching the house's rear window. Inside they could see agent Marcelle and David sitting with two other men at a table in what looked like a small office or den.

Polar gave Mystic a wry grin. "Bingo."

Inside that small office lined with tall wood paneling that hid secret closets, David Ramirez was meeting with GSA agent Devante Marcelle, Bureau Commander Johnson, and another FBI agent.

The room was quiet, with the only window covered by a blind that was turned down. They had expected agent Marcelle to bring them news, and he had a lot of it.

Agent Marcelle slapped a stack of files on the table and placed a notebook beside them. Johnson and all the weary, grizzled FBI agent all looked to him questioningly.

Agent Marcelle opened the notebook and found a file only he knew the password to. The screen came to life with mug shots of several people, among them a seemingly benign-looking train yard worker and a few scientists.

"There is your enemy," agent Marcelle said.

The men looked more closely at the screen.

"What you have found will finally help us bring this group to justice," the GSA agent said. The television screen flicked, the screen enlarged to a picture of Stanley Bennett as he looked before becoming Polar.

"They've infiltrated government buildings' security systems," Marcelle added. "They're still pretty much obscure to us because of their random attacks. We have tracked them over the past few days and have gotten this Intel on them." He sharpened the resolution of the screen. "We have no idea what their motives are, their affiliations, or of their funding. I've given them the name the Chaos. They're just causing problems for our operatives, so I thought Chaos would be a fitting name right now. Polar, a.k.a. Stanley Bennett you see here was an assistant working on finding new resources of energy using a classified chemical called Nitroglesine. He is wanted for the death of Professor Ulysses Donald, Chief of Bio-Chemical Research."

The other men at the table gave the screen a long study.

"Because of the neglect by Professor Donald," Marcelle continued, "the Chief of Bio-Chemical Research, Stanley was exposed to the toxic gas. Outside their work station, the cold elements altered his body chromosomes to produce frigid temperatures."

He changed the screen to show another man, this one in more casual work coveralls. "This one was the former Michael Owens, now known as Demolisher. One day a train transporting the highly radioactive chemical uranium was stationed at his yard. Greed took over, and Michael Owens, thinking he could make a big score, stole some of the uranium. Not having the proper containment, the uranium somehow spilled onto his body. The uranium transformed his skin into an impervious hardness. He is wanted for extortion, racketeering, and illegal arms transportation."

The screen changed again, this time to the Daniel Everson image standing beside Demolisher.

"You might remember this one," Marcelle said, switching the screen to show Daniel Everson. "I do. He was born in Lexington Park City as Daniel Everson. Daniel's parents were killed by corrupt police officers looking to find drugs in their expensive car. The police planted it there. Corruption runs deep, we know."

There were a few grim nods from the agents.

"Daniel's father fought back as the officers battered the boy's mother right before his young eyes." Marcelle sighed. "They were both killed. Daniel simply disappeared after that. We don't have much on these two."

The screen image changed again, this time to beings no one had named, beings that others knew as Toroks.

"They might be part of a well-placed gang or mob," Marcelle guessed. He flicked the screen to a shot of Wraith Blade. "We have no information on her either."

The FBI agent sat back, still contemplating the screen. "How does the government's GSA top G-Man not have any information on Wraith Blade? You've been after her for some time now."

Marcelle nodded. "She has managed to elude me. We are using every resource to get her. She just seems to be one step ahead of us."

Commander Johnson scowled at the screen. "They have advanced surveillance. They knew timetables, codes, and security protocols," he nearly growled. "Let's find them. We better move fast on this. I don't know exactly what they are planning but with this type of equipment, anything is possible. Let's hit them hard and fast."

"Commander, we need a Special Weapons and Ops team," Marcelle said. "They have high-powered technological weapons that we have no defense against. They will crush us if we attack now."

"They're not the only ones with power," the Commander bit back. He reached beneath the table and pulled out a roll of blueprints. "Old school, boys," he said as he unrolled the prints on the table. There were several layers of the prints rolled together and he smoothed the top sheet. "This series of plans is key. We know they plan to attack the Ravager Clan."

The agents all leaned closer to the table, eyes following the blueprint lines that detailed a weapon unlike any of them had ever seen.

"We're not totally without resources," the Commander said. "I have a weapons detail all lined up, courtesy of your organization and the Army. Take a look at these. As soon as these new power weapons arrive, we can launch our attack against them and stop their crime wave."

Agent Marcelle gets a call. While talking on the phone, he looks tense and upset.

"Look I have to go, there is urgent GSA matters that I need to attend to now. "

After Commander Johnson had shown the blueprints to everyone, agent Marcelle and David leave the meeting in separate cars.

Across a few buildings, Mystic was also watching between the blind slats at the unrolling of those prints through binoculars. He lowered the glasses, lips twitching.

"It seems they know about us. They have pictures and they named us Chaos." He grinned. "I like that."

Polar was not amused. "They know about us? How? We've always been careful."

Wraith Blade stood nearby, conducting her own surveillance on the men in the safe house. She takes off following Agent Marcelle's car.

Mystic raised the binoculars to his eyes again, viewing what was going on at the office table at the safe house. "Looks like they have pictures of us doing that military and jewelry heist. Some yapping." He nodded. "But they are on to us."

Polar frowned into the distance, seeing one of the men at the house leave. "If they're planning something, we better let everyone else know."

"This could complicate our timetable if we have to worry about them, too," Mystic said.

Polar shook his head. "Mystic, no, we need to take care of this now ourselves."

"You're right, Polar. Let's get all the evidence." He looked around, not seeing Wraith Blade. "Guess it's me and you for this one."

At the safe house, the FBI agents and Commander Johnson were just stowing the blueprints in one of the built-in wooden closets when a shearing sound was heard from the front door. Not five seconds later Mystic and Polar filled the office doorway.

The agents backed up, reaching for the closets.

"What is this?" Commander Johnson ordered, one hand going to his sidearm.

One of the agents shook his head. "What? It's them."

Mystic grinned, stepping into the room. "Well, well, look here."

The second agent pawed at the nearest closet, trying to find the disguised latch. "Are you crazy?"

Polar stepped closer. "Funny, that with all your technology the very planet you protect is about to be overtaken. We have taken intense extremes to keep our activities out of your view, but I see you have discovered us. "

Mystic looked to the Commander who was leaned against the panel closet, the plans still in his hand as his other hand gripped his gun holster, jerking at the weapon frantically.

"Looks like they are about to plan some type of assault against us," Mystic said, eyeing the long roll of prints. "Well, we are about to eliminate all knowledge of us."

The Commander pulled his gun and fired, missing both intruders.

The agents took the moment to rip the closet doors open and snag two assault rifles.

Bullets sprayed the small office interior, shattering lights and the window, ripping down the blinds.

Mystic raised his hand and hexed the bullets assailing him. They stopped midair, hanging there.

The first agent threw the assault weapon aside and grabbed a high-powered hunting rifle – a backup piece – and opened fire.

Polar halted the onslaught of slugs and turned his palm on the agents. With a sudden burst of frigidity, the agents were frozen in place, inside to out, organs brittle in seconds.

"Not on my--!" The Commander tried to rush, but Polar sent a blast of cold at him.

The Commander stopped, frozen solid, his expression still one of shouting.

"Enough small talk," Mystic said. He went to the closet near the commander and grabbed the rolled prints from the man and other files inside the closet.

"Search everywhere," Polar said, flinging open another closet. "Then we'll flame the place."

Within seconds the office was emptied of every valuable piece of evidence and planted with incendiary devices. Satisfied, Polar and Mystic left the safe house, springing out of sight over the three-story building nearby.

Ten seconds later the safe house exploded into flames.

Back on the ship, Amara had time to think back on the incident in the forest with the hunters. It amazed her that such beauty as the deer could live beside such danger as that posed by the Torok. She looked over the Elandrys.

He stood at the view screen, watching night fall over the city far below them. The lights twinkled on in tall buildings, smaller lights zipping around as cars sped through the streets. He'd come so far, only to find the same trouble that haunted his home planet.

She'd traveled enough with him to know that. She didn't like to see worry in his strong features. She much preferred the contented look that made his eyes liven and his thoughts turn to shared interests. But, she also knew that the worlds were no safe haven. He knew that, too. "Are you prepared?"

He looked to her, broken from his internal reverie. "Huh?"

She stepped closer and gently touched his solemn face, tracing the faint crease of frown at the corner of his mouth. "Are you prepared? We have not long ago ended a lingering, devastating, and hard fought war. It took much out of both sides." She hoped he would grin, but his stony expression remained locked. "Carnage was not known to your people until the Toroks came," she said softly. "Many of your beloved people, friends, and family died before your very eyes, some even in your very arms."

She felt his skin bristle as his jaw set, his eyes hardening on the gaze out the window.

"Your home planet and all that you knew was almost completely destroyed." She let her finger slide down his jaw to his neck, tracing to his shoulder and arm. "We may be again on the beginning of another devastating war."

He nodded, his posture relaxing minutely. "You're right, of course." Some of the steeliness left his eyes. "I see the same signs now as they were on Sundaria before the invasion started. What if we are not able to stop it here?" He shook his head and she closed her arms around his, leaning to his side. "I came to space to get away from everything there for a while, hoping the exhilaration and discovery of the wide unknown expanses of space would drown away all that pain. I'm millions of galaxies and solar systems away," he said, his tone taking on the slight edge of defeat. "Still it has found me. It seems to have crept slowly up on me."

Elandrys turned to face her, seeing the hope and stout support in her eyes. "No... I don't know if I am ready. I was fighting for my – our – people's survival. We were trying to save our own lives. Honestly, I'm not over seeing so much bloodshed and death. If there is a Sundarian here," he said, looking back out the dark window that showed the vastness of the city below, "I know I must do everything to see it through, to save their life. If it's the Toroks, my duty is to stop them."

She let her temple rest against his arm, feeling the underlying strength within the muscles, knowing the power he harnessed both mentally and physically. They may need every bit of strength any of them had.

"New planet, peculiar people," she said quietly. "A man willing to risk his life for his people. I think that is honorable courage. Remember this one thing, Elandrys," she added, looking up at him. "I will never leave you, for anything. Whatever happens, I will go with you. I fight with you. If it's the Toroks, I agree with you to stop them."

He pulled her close to his side, knowing she meant every word, both spoken and unspoken playing in her eyes. He liked the subtle strength in her curves, the loyalty in her actions.

He knew they may well need everything both of them had to offer.

Back at the warehouse, the group formally known as Chaos disposed of the evidence against them. Polar, Mystic, and Demolisher joined the two Toroks awaiting them.

"It had been a productive day – one safe house gone and the FBI's carefully gathered evidence confiscated" says Polar grinning as he dropped the roll of blueprints onto the table and looked at Zevyn and Kevlar.

"One less toy in their arsenal," he said with a hearty chuckle.

The Toroks both looked to the collection of cameras and files Mystic and Demolisher sorted through. Outside the city was quieter as night fell.

"What's all this?" Kevlar asked. He watched Mystic examine one of the cameras.

Polar crossed his arms. "They think we are international terrorist wanting to sell arms or maybe trading secrets."

The news didn't sit well with Mystic despite the evidence they'd stolen. "Other agencies may now be aware of us."

Demolisher examined one of the files, nodding as he read. "Yeah, like Wraith's friend."

Mystic sat back on the sofa and laced his fingers behind his head, grinning broadly at their stash. "We took all the evidence we could find. I think we should call ourselves Chaos, thanks to the agents naming us. It's got a good ring to it; fearsome yet enigmatic."

Zevyn nodded. "Everyone agreed to the name?"

Polar and Mystic grunted their approval, attention still on the evidence dumped on the table.

"Good," Zevyn said. "Now we need to find a stable power source. Ours is running down and we don't want to get caught in a weak state."

Mystic looked to him. "I can try to get money from some of the diamonds we stole." He laughed. "Nothing holds value like gem-stones and gold."

"That'll hold us for a while." Polar stood and looked to Demolisher and Mystic. "Until then, we've got other matters to attend to."

Within moments the three super-humans had left the warehouse. The Toroks looked to each other.

Zevyn grinned cruelly. "Commander will be please with us finding this planet. These natives are so easy to manipulate, but we do need them. We definitely need to look into the power of their sun and water resources."

Kelvar carefully sorted the files and clicked off the digital camera. He fingered one of the removable flash drives. "It's a lot of damaging evidence before us." He nodded. "These humans have their own agenda, and so far, it works for us." He looked steadily to Zevyn. "What do you think Polar, Demolisher, Wraith, and Mystic will do when they find out they are helping us destroy their planet?"

"What could they do?" Zevyn's tone held no worry. "When we are finished, with our power and resources, they and the planets will be totally destroyed. We need to get communications up and running. That is the only way we can really conquer Earth."

"I wish we had more time to study this planet. We were defeated on Sundaria," Kevlar recalled. "What if these natives, too, have some secret weapon that could defeat us? We still don't really know how the Sundarians won."

Zevyn wasn't concerned. "We have seen Earth's military capabilities. I wouldn't agonize too much. I know the unlimited weapons of Toria can overpower this planet." He made a tight fist with his hand, shaking it slightly as if to challenge an unseen enemy. "This planet is predestined to be ours."

CHAPTER SIX

Wraith Blade stood atop a six-story building, looking over the city as night fell.

So he was truly there. She hadn't forgotten him or the days and nights they'd shared.

Long-dead feelings for GSA Agent Devante Marcelle suddenly surfaced inside her, threatening to split her calloused heart open with fresh emotions.

She closed her eyes, feeling the cool breeze swirl her hair around her as her mind's eye brought back that glimpse of him. It wasn't the same; nothing could ever be the same. They were now on different – opposite – sides of right and wrong.

Her memories invaded her senses and she could once again feel the warm summers in China as they'd grown up together. She smiled a bit, lips unable to refuse the happiness they had known as children. That little Wuyuan village seemed so far away now.

It had been more than their ages, their feelings of isolation, and how different they both were from the children around them. She was a half-Chinese, half-Venezuelan, a Latina girl growing up in the farmlands near the village, with no one like her. Devante was also unlike any of them there. His skin was dark and he was from America – an African-American – the first she had ever seen. She thought he was beautiful.

She smiled as she let the memory take her far away from the city below. And, he had thought she was beautiful, too.

From their initial meeting they made their differences what made them cling to each other.

Less of a smile pulled at her lips. It was a long time ago, a time when neither of them wanted to learn to fight.

But they had, through martial arts and more, always by each other's side.

Her eyes opened. Devante was unlike anyone she'd ever met, even now. The stars overhead winked on in the heavy night sky, reminding her of over stars in a wide cobalt-black sky of another time.

Her memory came back in force and for a moment she could almost feel the stray water drops of the waterfall at the mountainside of that Chinese village. She and Devante had always been together.

At times she wanted those days back, to make new memories. Her gaze focused below on the city lights trying to rival the brilliant starlight. A chill swept up her spine.

A sudden stronger gust of wind swept the building top and she turned to see a small heliplane descend across the rooftop.

She was ready to leap off when the plane's door swung open and Devante Marcelle stepped out.

"Angela!" he called when he saw her. "Please wait!"

All her memories flooded away and Wraith Blade, no longer that Angela from the China farmlands, glared at him. "Who calls? Is this my lover Devante?" She laughed cruelly. "You've come to rescue me?"

He crossed the rooftop and slowed as he saw the anger in her face. "I'm trying to get you to stop this foolishness, Angela," he said, assessing her mood. "You don't have to go through with any of this. Come with me and I'll make sure—-"

"What?" she nearly spat, closing the distance more between them. "Make sure of what, Devante? You'll go easy on me? So I see you haven't said you know me. You don't. Not anymore." A thin smile crossed her lips. "What would your police buddies think about you helping the most-hunted assassin in the world? Helping a criminal is a crime, isn't it?"

He shook his head slowly. "Helping someone you love is not."

She didn't want it to, but seeing him again made something in her revive, something she'd spent a long time burying. "I needed you." She didn't like how soft her voice was, but she couldn't keep the choking emotion from her words. "Why did you leave?"

"You wanted a life that I disagreed with," he said in a quiet tone. "I'm trying my best to help you. Forget the past; you know you can start over, and I'll help you. You know I will." He smiled more. "Your family loves you. I love you. I just want you to see what you're doing is going to get you killed if you don't stop. Nothing in this world matters to me but you."

He still had a way with her, even by those few words. Wraith Blade didn't want them to, but the words pierced the callousness of her heart. She quickly turned away, knowing if she didn't, she'd be rooted to the spot and succumb to anything he said.

"Stop," she said, summoning her resolve. "Stop talking. If you don't leave now I'm going to kill you. Leave me alone forever."

She turned her head slowly, her face stony as she watched him out of the corner of her eye. She drew her sword, mentally shoring up her steely facade.

She noted he didn't reach for his gun. She almost wished he would. It would make this so much easier for her.

Devante watched her fingers tighten on the sword hilt; saw the tenseness in her lips. His hand balled as he swallowed uncomfortably.

With catlike reflexes, she spun and lunged at him.

He stepped back as her hand shot out, flinging a knockout pellet in her other hand at him.

His last sight of her as he sunk to the rooftop was the shimmering image of her watching him, unmoving. He fell unconscious, where dreams and memories eclipsed reality.

Wraith Blade barely saw agent Marcelle fall before she leaped to the next building a story higher than the one she'd been on. She turned and looked back.

Agent Marcelle was laying still, his chest rising and falling with breathing. She didn't dare close her eyes, knowing the memories would flood her soul.

"I love you, too," she said softly, and then turned away. "I always will."

Devante Marcelle was from her past. Now, she had a loose end in David Ramirez to tie up.

She raced on to meet Mystic, Polar, Demolisher and the Toroks, leaving her past far behind in the inky night.

At least, she tried to leave it.

Elandrys and Amara flew the ship silently over the city, watching the pinpoints of streetlamps and apartment lights flick on as dark descended. The hunters from the forest were still on their minds, and although the people of Earth were more fragile as species, they did have their artificial armor.

Elandrys looked to Amara at his side. "The people of this planet seem to be well-armed and somewhat violent for such a timid species," he said. "We need to maintain a low profile. I have been attacked twice." He watched a few cars stop at a traffic light below between the tall buildings. "And I'm still without answers."

She nodded. "Weaker animals often find a means of protection when they feel vulnerable. I suggest you change into your Sundarian protective suit."

He glanced to the items they'd found and brought aboard. "These ship parts are from Toria. If the Toroks are planning to attack Earth, there should be more here." He looked back to the city below them. "Hiding in the shadows, naturally."

"I agree. It's not their normal behavior to travel so lightly. Usually they like a large group. They may be here in mass numbers, keeping to the shadows, as you say."

His expression grew troubled as he watched the city blocks pass below them. "Amara, scan for abnormal transmissions broadcasting into space," he said. "We can still track the Sundarian energy source as well. You will need to block any of Earth air defenses or scans of us. We need to remain hidden from them."

She nodded. "Right."

The Amara continued to fly over the city, attempting to stay hidden in the low lying clouds. Below the sleek ship, the city went about its usual nightlife.

People bustled around, deals made and parties underway, everyone oblivious to the alien ship just out of sight. No one on the ground was aware of the struggle between otherworlders underway.

Elandrys knew Amara was recording everything they saw, from the cars and people to the stray cats in the darkened alleys. No one in Lexington Park City was aware of the possible trouble brewing.

Amara looked up from her scanning. "I've gotten a location on communication equipment not of Earth origin."

He nodded to her. "Let's go."

Within moments they had found the remote location that the scan had indicated. It was on the edge of the city, the air laced by large cable antennas. The abandoned lot had once been a warehouse for auto parts, but now it was more of a graveyard of unwanted and obsolete half-junked cars.

Too old and outdated to be used as salvage parts, the cars lined the weedy lot like automotive skeletons, blocking most of the view of the interior of the yard, but inside that yard a block building stood. It was twenty feet square and many of the antennas above were attached to two of its three utility poles.

Elandrys and Amara gave the yard a quick glimpse as they rode the airways in, hovering over the yard a moment to get their bearings. Not much of the streetlights illuminated the yard, and long shadows cast over the metal strewn ground and block building. The yard looked to be empty of people and dogs and only the muted sounds of a train passing further down the street could be heard.

Elandrys and Amara landed and looked around the car-lined yard. Sure enough, the signal they'd picked up on the scanner was correct. Behind the building a roll-up door was open and a small utility room was exposed. Inside were workbenches, all laden with transmission equipment.

Elandrys gave the tables a swift study. "This communications transmitter is working through a complex integrated network." He nodded to where the wires were patched through the wall near one of the utility poles outside. "It appears someone has been here recently."

Amara nodded in agreement. "These humans have not developed this type of technology, based on my recent scans of all their communications equipment." She stepped closer to one of the programs running on a transmitter. "They haven't developed this level of capability yet."

He was looking at a receiver. "This is not Sundarian technology either."

She didn't touch any of the instruments, but her eyes took in every detail. "I am not too familiar with the Toroks' communications devices, but this could be their technology."

He gave the next table of devices a careful study. "The Toroks are here and they are likely planning to invade this planet. I am sure of it now." He leaned over the table and found the connections to the outer wall. "I'm going to disable it. Hopefully that will bring the Toroks back to try and fix it. We can see what we are facing then."

Amara spun around as the sounds of footsteps reached her ears. She looked out the roll-up door, seeing a few shadows change in the yard. "Humans are approaching."

As she spoke, a dark form appeared at the corner of the open doorway, raising his rifle as he spotted them. "Hey, you two get away from there!"

Behind him stepped two more guards, all armed and ready.

Elandrys turned to face the three guards. "Please, we are just looking at this equipment."

The first guard waved the barrel of his rifle to indicate them to move out of the room. "I said move!"

Amara pivoted more to face the guards. "We are trying to see if you are about to be invaded."

The first guard chuckled. "Invading us? Get that?" he said, nudging his closest fellow guard before turning back to Amara. "How do we know you are not the ones invading us?"

Elandrys took a step forward. "I assure you we are not. Please, if you will just listen to us," he implored. "There may be people here getting ready to do harm your planet."

The second guard grew impatient. "They're crazy," he spat, his posture bracing. "Take them down!"

A hail of bullets fired on Elandrys and Amara, but the shots were careful, as the guards didn't want to damage the equipment behind the two. The aims were careful, and each bullet missed as they bounced off the block walls at chest height.

In that split second of cautious fire, Elandrys charged the three men. He caught the first by the wrist holding the rifle and shoved it up as the guard fired. The Sundarian sent a quick palm cuff under his chin and the man's head snapped back. A rift of shots sprayed the roll-up door of the building, a few hitting the overhead cables and antennas.

The other two guards rushed Elandrys, pelting gunfire, but the Sundarian crashed their attempts with a series of expert punches and kicks to their chests and necks. The two guards swore and fell back, but one scrambled to his feet. He flung two kicks at Elandrys' abdomen, missing each time, and Elandrys double-punched him in the face. The guard fell and lay still.

"Look out!" Amara called.

Elandrys looked up as the huge cable antennas tumbled down, pinning the fallen guards. The men cried out as the heavy metal trapped them. Elandrys and Amara pulled the antennas off the men, who were now unconscious.

Amara looked around at the scene. It would surely draw attention. Already shouts and a faraway siren could be heard in the dark. She quickly transformed into her ship self and swept Elandrys away into the night.

Also in that night an otherwise jaded GSA Agent Devante Marcelle's thoughts hung as old memories draped in the twilight of dream and waking. Sitting at the edge of the building rooftop when he had awaken from Angela's gas pellet, he was always haunted by memories of her, his Angela – now Wraith Blade – and their past together.

Somewhere in their history, a time long ago yet not forgotten by either, simpler days and nights waited to be revisited. She never forgot their first kiss over stolen pastries in the moonlight or how soft the grass felt beneath their bodies in intimate pleasure. It was a first for both of them.

And sometimes, in Marcelle's yearnings, he feared those days were all past.

But he doesn't forget, and his thoughts and memories – like hers – hang in the night, shared by time.

Neither does Angela, now Wraith Blade and enemy, forget...

Her reality with mine was unreal, influencing
All my reasoning, every moment together.
I often see her in my slumber; her scent lingers with me for days.
Her compassionate voice awakens my deepest slumber and it brings
comfort to my soul, even when she is not there.
I hear her smoothly whispered "I love you" in my ear.
This is all before I ever knew she existed.
It makes all the little moments precious.
Being together is pure ecstasy.
There is no other place like it in the world, with her.

My skin absorbs his every touch, sweet kisses and soft caresses.

He is the sweetest, strongest taste ever savored.

True love was never meant to say goodbye

It should never make you weep.

You are my dream

The only one that I can ever be in love with,

My every reason for breathing.

CHAPTER SEVEN

Wraith Blade stood alone and silent in the night atop a roof that overlooked the Velasquez apartment. She has had it under surveillance for ten minutes now, long enough to know who was inside and what needed to be done.

She slowly turned as Mystic, Demolisher, and Zevyn as they joined her. Their attention was on the target unit, too.

Mystic grinned as he watched the few figures move inside the sliding glass door behind the small balcony that hung outside the exterior wall near the Velasquez living room. "There he is," he said, watching David move inside the house in the lamplight. He nodded with satisfaction. "Perfect."

Demolisher crossed his arms over his massive chest. "Is he alone in there?"

Wraith Blade shook her head. "A woman is in there also."

Zevyn's lips curled a grimace. "It doesn't matter. Let's go."

Mystic said a chant and they all glided to Mrs. Velasquez balcony. They alighted to the balcony just outside the Velasquez living room and Demolisher crashed through the double-paned glass balcony door. The noise resonated through the neighborhood and started several dogs barking.

At the sudden disturbance, David was already on his feet, but startled Mrs. Velasquez was still sitting on the couch with a museum directory in her hands. She flinched as the four known as Chaos shoved through the balcony glass door, then gasped as they advanced on her.

David spun to look at each of them in turn, knowing full well who they were. "You? No! No!" He put a hand to his side before remembering he was unarmed. "How did you find me?"

Demolisher gave him a snarling smile. "So it's our little spy. Well, well. Isn't that fitting?"

Mrs. Velasquez tried to shakily get to her feet, but it took her a moment to comprehend the villains who had stormed them. "David, what's going on? Who are these people?"

Zevyn stepped closer to her. "David knows who we are, but if you should know, we are Chaos!"

"Run!" David yelled to her. "Get out!"

Demolisher grabbed Mrs. Velasquez as she tried to bolt from the room. He held her up by her collar and leaned close to her terrified face, chuckling as she futilely squirmed and clawed at his large fist.

Zevyn laughed. "David here likes to stick his nose in other peoples' business." He threw David a glare. "We'll teach you to stay out of our affairs." He glanced back at Mrs. Velasquez, who was kicking and trying to tear away Demolisher's hand on her. "You will suffer and tonight you will die!"

"You will never get away with what you are planning!" David promised, shaking his head. "We will stop you!"

Chaos lunged at David before David could move. Demolisher dropped Mrs. Velasquez and grabbed David. He tossed him into the far wall, where he crashed and slid down to the floor, leaving cracked drywall at the impact. With a single raise of his hand, Polar froze the door, locking them inside the apartment with an icy grip.

Mrs. Velasquez got to her feet and began to scream, but Mystic chant raised her in the air and hexed her throat. With her vocal cords paralyzed, and she pawed desperately at her neck, eyes widening in fear as Mystic let her drop hard to the floor.

David struggled to his feet, shaking off the toss, and reached into a wall cupboard for his backup handgun. No sooner had he raised the handgun and cocked it than Wraith Blade, Demolisher, and Zevyn rushed him. They forced him to the floor with pounding fists and a few kicks.

Seeing his agony, Mrs. Velasquez grabbed the nearest table lamp she could reach and tried to throw it. Demolisher swiftly moved towards her and grabbed her. Demolisher flung her across the room with a brutal kick. Her back hit the china cabinet, which wavered and then toppled down on her. The heavy piece of furniture crashed like an imploded building on her, breaking bones and china and glassware.

Mrs. Velasquez screamed as chards of glass and ceramic cut into her. The weight of the cabinet crushed her ribs. She wheezed out a scream of pain as the sharp glass pierced her skin and face.

David tried to help her, but he'd curled into the fetal position as kicks and fists rained down on him. Through the blood dripping into his eyes he could see Mrs. Velasquez cease to move beneath the heavy china cabinet.

"No..." he gasped as a wicked kick to his ribs made him wince and lose his breath. He coughed, blood spurting with saliva as he tried to speak. "No..."

He heard a click of a weapon and then the Torok's weapon barrel angled into his blurry view. There was a white flash, and then the blackness of death.

Zevyn stepped back from the pulpy mass that had been David Ramirez. He looked to the others. "Search the place."

Far above the madness that was sucking the life out of the two people in that apartment, Amara hovered in the night skies.

Inside the ship, Amara and Elandrys were consulting the instruments and monitors. They had been monitoring the readings for a while now and it was undeniable.

"I'm picking up a surge of Sundarian energy again," Amara said.

He joined her at her console and studied the screen she was viewing. "Let's get there. We need to see what's going on here. My curiosity is overwhelmed."

She nodded. "Do you think the Sundarians could have chased the Toroks here?" she said.

He sighed, nodding sadly at the painful memories. "The war has been over for some time now. Surely they would have returned back to Sundaria, not come to Earth. Besides, the Sundarians are not capable of traveling here or launching an attack against the Toroks if they are here."

Amara considered this for a moment. "You are right. If we must help this planet stand against an attack of the Toroks, than we will. If not, they may surely perish. However, we are here alone. We have no one to help us defeat the Toroks."

She made an adjustment on the screen, but it did little to pinpoint any new information. "Then let's continue searching for answers. I am still tracking the energy. It's there."

For several long moments Amara made minute adjustments to the instruments, seeking any sign of Torok activity to help them home-in on the best places to search. It took a while to get any useful results, but suddenly Amara smiled, waving Elandrys closer when he'd gone back to his own study.

"Here," she said, indicating a small blip on another screen. A thin line stretched across the grid representing Lexington Park. "Energy trails."

He leaned closer to examine the scene. "Let's go."

Within moments Amara had descended enough for Elandrys and her to hover in the peaceful neighborhood just a few streets from the Velasquez' apartment. They easily found their way through the dark skies and down the brightly lit streets until they were just across from the wide glass door at the balcony. By now the dogs had ceased barking. Both Elandrys and Amara frowned as they considered the curtains blowing oddly in through the broken glass of the balcony door.

"That glass opening is not open. It's smashed. Something has happened there," Elandrys said as they observed the exterior of the apartment. "That glass is broken from the outside in."

Amara nodded. Amara lowered to the balcony level and opened her hatch door, and then Elandrys leaped into the apartment. Amara transformed and followed behind.

The apartment was in shambles as they carefully entered through the splintered sliding glass door at the balcony. Among the overturned furniture and pillaged drawers and cabinets, David and Mrs. Velasquez's bodies lay on the floor, unmoving.

Elandrys sensed the imminent death of the two life forms known as humans. He examined the air particles with a device of Sundarian technology as Amara moved about the room. Then Elandrys saw a discarded Torok weapon not far from the man's body, he bent down to examine it.

"Amara, two human bodies," he said, glancing first to the crushed woman under the cabinet and then to David's beaten form against the wall. "This is Sundarian energy, but the weapons are from the Toroks. Torok technology and a Sundarian on Earth." He shook his head. "What have we stumbled into?"

Elandrys started to try and move the broken china cabinet but stopped his motion; a muffled sound came to the hallway just outside the door. Amara glanced quickly to him. "Elandrys, someone is coming to the door. Let's get out!" Elandrys takes the discarded Torok weapon and places it in his side pouch.

Maria opened the door to her parents' apartment and stepped in, expecting a warm hug and friendly greeting. Instead, she saw a very large, well-muscled man and a strange dressed woman standing living room. She blinked at him in shock.

She managed to ask, "Who are you?"

Before Elandrys could answer, Maria realized the disarray of the house and saw the overturned case. She took a step and to her horror, saw her mother lying beneath the heavy case, unmoving. Maria gasped and looked to Elandrys, and then her eye caught another figure on the floor. Immediately she saw David.

"No..." Her gaze snapped to the Sundarian. "No! What did you do to him?"

She rushed to David's limp body and knelt. Her fingers probed his neck, finding no pulse. She looked up at Elandrys as he took half a step, confusion on his face at what to say to this earthling.

Maria leaped to her feet and rushed him. "You bastard!"

Before he could react, she threw a sudden abrupt punch he barely dodged. Despite the tears forming in her eyes, she grabbed an overturned lamp and swung it at him. He backed up, avoiding the following desperate lunges she made at him.

"What did you do to them?" she screamed. She threw the lamp away and grabbed a fire iron when she reached the fireplace as Elandrys backed up. "Who are you? Get away from them!"

She charged him with the fire iron raised over her head. She brought it down with what she hoped to be a solid thud on his chest, but he knocked the iron away and deflected her attack.

"Stop! "said Amara. "We wish you no harm. "

Maria did not pay any attention to Amara. Maria recoiled for another strike attempt, but Elandrys caught the rod and shoved it back, making Maria stumble backwards. She pulled the iron out of his hand and swung it wide, then followed with a roundhouse kick to his sternum.

He knocked her foot away and ripped the iron rod from her hands and tossed it to a side wall. The movement made Maria stumble nearly to her knees and Elandrys and Amara took the moment to dash to the balcony door.

Maria only saw him dive out of the balcony and into thin air. She fought back tears and raced after them.

Outside she just caught the glimpse of the two figures, the woman transformed and a ship appeared, the man leaped on and the ship sped away, dissolving into the night sky. She couldn't believe her eyes, but she didn't linger. She turned and ran back to her mother and knelt. She put a hand to her mother's neck and felt the shallow pulse there.

"Oh, good..."

She quickly went to David and dropped to her knees.

"Hang on, David," she said as she frantically felt again for a pulse at his neck. Getting none, she pulled her phone from her back pocket and dialed. "Yes, Nine-One-One? I have an emergency!" She hastily gave the dispatcher her address, then left the phone on beside her beloved. "They're on they're way, David. Stay with me!"

She put an ear to his chest, and then, hearing nothing, cupped the nape of his neck in her hand and tilted his head back. She pinched his nose closed with one hand and lowered her mouth to his open lips. For several minutes she tried to breathe life into him, trying not to sob as his still body refused air. She sniffed and lowered his head.

"David...David... Oh, God, please don't die! I love you, David!"

She sat up on her knees and put one hand on his chest and covered it with her other palm and pressed down. With quick, even pumps, she tried to restart his stalled heart. Each movement brought despair closer to her heart. "Please, David... Please..."

For several long, agonizing moments she worked. Finally, in the distance, she heard an ambulance siren. She cried out through the tears now running down her checks, blurring her view of David's blood-soaked face and chest. "Somebody help me! Please!"

She stopped attempting to resuscitate him and pulled him into her arms. He was warm, but fading. She held him closer, tightly against her chest as if her heart could restart his through sheer desperation and love.

By the time the ambulance EMT and police officers came through the open apartment door five minutes later, David was dead. Maria's heartbroken face greeted them as she sobbed.

Maria didn't quite comprehend the order of events after that. Paco her brother was suddenly there, as was Camille, but she didn't recall them arriving. Her mother was swiftly dislodged from the case and carefully attended to by the EMT team.

Maria watched numbly as her mother was put on a gurney and taken out the doorway. David was also moved, covered with a white blanket that quickly stained red.

Paco said something about going with the ambulance. Maria only nodded as Camille held her.

Once the EMT was gone and some of the officers had left, Maria got a better look at the torn up living room. What happened here? she wondered. That man, that woman with the odd clothes...

"It's going to be okay, Maria honey," Camille said.

Maria didn't believe her.

One of the sterner looking officers approached them, a caustic look on his face. "Which one of you is Maria Velasquez?"

Maria sighed shakily. "I am."

He nodded. "I'm GSA Agent Marcelle. I'm sorry you had to be here, Ms. Velasquez." He looked to Camille. "Can you please step away while I speak privately with your friend here?"

Camille didn't want to leave Maria at a time like this, but she nodded, giving Maria a quick hug before carefully stepping over the lamp on the floor.

GSA agent Marcelle cleared his throat. "The FBI is going to have questions for you, but I can tell you a little bit they can't."

"I...I don't understand all this," she said just above a whisper.

"David was secretly working with us," he told her. "We don't know how they found out about David, but we will do everything we can to find who did this. I will have every man on this, Ms. Velasquez. Trust me."

"Maria, please," she said.

"Okay, Maria it is."

She looked around at the wreckage as he said more, but she wasn't entirely listening. The apartment was in shambles, with the fireplace tools lying all over, some with blood on them. One of these tools suddenly sharpened in her focus and she realized it wasn't a fireplace implement at all. It was a knife, rather, a throwing dagger.

Her thoughts raced as her heart broke. "Why didn't David tell me about this? Who was he investigating?"

"David probably didn't want you to worry. We cannot tell you a lot about the investigation, as most of it is classified," he said, watching her wiping her face with a blood-stained hand. "I know one of the members of this crime organization. They are very ruthless."

She shook her head. "How could this happen? We were going to get married."

Camille took this a signal to rejoin her friend. "I know this is hard," she said consolingly, putting an arm around Maria. "But the FBI is going to do everything possible." She looked to GSA agent Marcelle, who nodded in agreement. "I'll ask around at the office to see what I can find out."

Maria looked over to where one of the officers was squatting and retracing in thicker white the outline of where David's body had been on the floor.

That was all that she had left of him. That hollow outline.

She started to cry, turning her face to Camille's shoulder.

Camille pulled her into a tight embrace, patting her back as she gently murmured, "You go ahead and cry, Maria."

Far above the city falling into a darker night, Elandrys and Amara lingered in the clouds as they watched the scene below. They'd already saw the EMTs carry out David's dead body. Around the ambulance the squad cars with the flashing lights and now silenced sirens stood a few onlookers, but other than that, the city went about its normal nightlife.

Elandrys sighed, frowning. "There was a fight there. It looked to be at least three to four people. We probably cannot go back there." He watched one of the squad cars slowly drive away, followed by the ambulance, which now turned on its siren. "There are too many people gathering, and a woman inside the housing unit thinks I killed someone. She may report us to their authorities."

Amara nodded, tilting her head as she listened to an earpiece. "Scanning some of the many conversations... Everything sounds confusing. They are questioning people, but nobody saw anything. They only heard loud noises and screaming, dogs barking, things breaking. All we really have is the signal to follow."

He nodded. "I see. Scan for the signal, Amara. That's all we have to go on right now. They still do not know about that."

She listened for a moment, switching frequencies until she finally got a tendril of something. "I'm now getting a weak signal. It's moving."

He didn't like what he'd seen below. "This is not the actions of a Sundarian. We would not kill senselessly. What does this man have to do with a Sundarian?"

She had no answers. "I agree, but how do you explain the Sundarian reading I'm getting? A Sundarian with Torok weapons killing humans."

The neighborhood below quieted as the sirens faded into the maze of city streets. Down there, Elandrys knew, there was a brave, spirited young woman with a broken heart. "Continue to track that signal even though it is weak," he said to Amara. "We need to find out who this person is. I don't believe it's a Sundarian."

CHAPTER EIGHT

The sterile environment of Lexington Park Hospital seemed stark in the late night as Maria, Mr. Velasquez, Paco, and Camille waited. Mrs. Velasquez had been taken into surgery three hours ago and then set up in a room afterwards. The surgeon had been brief and to the point: the outlook was not good. They'd not heard much since.

Maria had held back long enough. Watching her mother hooked up to assorted medical instruments that regulated her breathing and monitored her heartbeat, with I.V. lines running into both arms, was more than she could tolerate. Her mother's pale face was nearly covered with bandages, too. Maria stormed out into the hallway. Behind her, she heard the door open, but she didn't stop.

"Maria!" her father called. "Maria...!"

She stopped and spun around. "What?" she snapped out.

"What, Daddy?"

He frowned at the turmoil and anger in her face. He knew it too well. "I don't like that look in your eyes. That usually means you're getting ready to do something you may regret."

She gestured to the room behind him. "Mom is lying in there beaten half to death. There is nothing I'm going to regret when I find out who did this."

"Let the police handle this," he said slowly. "It's their job. Actions have consequences; are you ready to face the bad consequences when you make bad choices?"

She nearly laughed.

"Absolutely yes! What did Mom do to deserve this?" A nurse quickly approached from behind Mr. Velasquez and looked to each of them. "This is a hospital. Please lower your voices."

Maria turned on her. "Shut the hell up!" Before Mr. Velasquez could admonish her, Maria bolted down the hallway. "Maria! Maria!"

Tears of anger and helplessness stung her eyes as Maria raced back to the Community Center. She quickly made her way through the dark, empty halls that echoed with her quick steps. Within seconds of opening the metal locker in the changing room, she was transformed.

Now, in place of the helpless Maria Velasquez stood Onyx, a sleek blue and purple clad figure that could do something about the attack.

In moments she was back on the streets, keen eyes trained on any movement beneath the city lights and clouded skies. Her first target was a lowlife lying in wait as a few older teens loitered at a park. She first dropped down from her vantage point of a three-story building and confronted the teens about being out so late, and then, as the kids ran home, grilled the would-be attacker. He was a low level thief who shook when she spoke to him and in the end, after firing questions at him, Onyx let him go.

"I need a better plan," she murmured as the unkempt thief ran off. She glanced around, searching out any movement in the darkened corners of the park.

"I need a systematic search of all these criminals, this network of lowlifes. Someone must know something about that man who attacked Mom and David."

She looked down at the throwing dagger in her hand. It was the only piece of evidence she had from the crime scene of her parents' apartment. It was Asian in style, with a double blade and aerodynamic design. The police had overlooked it at the apartment.

"Sorry, Daddy," she said as she took off again. "I'm not leaving this for the authorities."

Over the next few hours she rounded up half a dozen mid-level criminals and a few hoodlums and interrogated them, sometimes with threats, sometimes merely by dropping down in their midst, startling them. None had seen the dagger. No one knew anything about the man she described as the attacker in the apartment. And no one was able to help.

She finally leapt to the nearest four-story building as dawn timidly peeked over the city limits. It looked different to her; maybe not the buildings and usual early morning traffic and commuters. Something else.

She crouched at the rooftop edge and focused her vision on the faces of the people on the sidewalks. They all looked different, guilty, like they were hiding something. She blinked and looked again. It was still there, that thinly veiled guilt that everyone – from the women in their heels and business suits to the men on cell phones carrying briefcase to high-power elite office buildings – wore in their eyes.

"Has it always been this way?" Onyx asked no one as she watched the traffic below increase as the sun topped the skyline.

"What can everyone be guilty of? Compliance?

Greed? Are they all so eager to look the other way when a crime is committed? Are we all so guilty, to some degree?" She stood straight and looked down upon the city waking up.

Maybe, for the first time, she was seeing the world for what it really was.

Across the city at the docks, the sun was also rising over the Lexington Park warehouses. In one of these, Chaos had gathered and was now taking stock of their collective haul.

Milling around the amounting armaments were both Toroks, Wraith Blade, Mystic, Demolisher, and Polar. Their recent separate scrapes with the authorities had only whetted their appetites for greater destruction. Zevyn nodded in satisfaction as he estimated the equipment.

"These will come in handy when we weaponize them!"

Wraith Blade sidled up to him and dangled an intricately wired device before him. "I have the module for the transporter boost."

He made to grab at it, but she pulled it away, laughing when he scowled.

"Not so fast, hot shot," she cooed, stepping back to the computers.

Kelvar watched her sweep her hair from her face as she leaned over to read a computer screen. After admiring her backside for a moment, he turned to where Mystic was seated at another terminal. "How soon can our ship be repaired and our communications restored?"

Mystic tapped at the keyboard for a moment. "Soon. The diagnostics are finished for your communications." He turned in his chair to look at the Torok. "We need an intergalactic transceiver for it to work."

Wraith Blade printed a readout of the diagnostics and took them with her to the other end of the warehouse.

Demolisher glanced between her and Mystic and then nodded to Zevyn. "What are you guys planning with all this?"

"I know you are looking for that one big score, but this will be bigger than that," Zevyn said. "Total conquest. Once we accent your planets energy to power our weapons, we will be the most powerful beings on this planet. No one would be able to stop us."

Demolisher was skeptical. "You got a grudge?"

"You could say that."

Kelvar sent Demolisher a pointed look. "You were there. You saw what it did to our ship. We're...what's the word? Oh, grateful, yeah, for you and Polar and Wraith Blade hiding us from your authorities after the crash, but we've got bigger plans than being mere survivors on your planet."

"The ship you found us crashed in was only a cruiser vessel," Zevyn explained. "A transport ship. While we were at war, it was used to bring supplies. We didn't have a full weapons armament. We were chased into space after being spotted and had unloaded our supplies. We were desperate. No food, very little energy. The Sundarians turned away, but our guidance systems were destroyed.

We drifted until we found a habitable planet. It was by chance we found this planet."

"This planet has vast resources," Kelvar said. "Once our communications are functional we can send our location to our planet for full armaments."

With a nod to Zevyn, Kelvar started for the far bay door. As both Toroks left, the other three of Chaos glanced at each other.

"Polar," Demolisher said, "I think we need to keep an eye on Wraith."

Polar nodded slightly. "She knows a cop. She gets rickety when he is around. I don't trust her."

Mystic waved off their suspicions. "Don't worry, Demolisher. Wraith has always been loyal."

Demolisher leaned forward in his chair. "Yeah, Mystic,but what if she double-crosses us? I don't feel she--"

"Look, I have faith in her," Mystic cut in. "That's all that matters. I'm not worried about Wraith. I'm more concerned about these Toroks."

"Why?" Demolisher asked. Mystic shrugged. "Where do we fit in their plan exactly? If they bring more of their people to our planet, take over the planet, what's really left for us? I mean, these are people from another planet. How can we know we can trust them? I have been recalibrating their calculations; something is not right about it."

"Well, they seemed to be totally honest with us," Demolisher decided, looking to the Toroks as they inspected the equipment at the bay door. He turned back to Mystic and Polar. "But you think they're using us?"

Mystic rubbed his shoulder. "I don't have any evidence yet, but there is something more to the stories they are telling is. That's something I don't like."

Polar nodded slowly. "Mystic is right. We should keep a real close eye on them. If Wraith messes up, we kill her. Simple. Same for these Toroks."

"I don't have a problem with any of you. Even Wraith," Mystic said. "We just need to be careful. Watch your backs, is all I'm saying. Okay, now let's get back to work. Time is precious."

Amara hovered overhead as Elandrys kept a careful watch, making his way to the warehouse he suspected held answers to his questions. He didn't like the idea of a Sundarian on Earth without his knowledge, but he had to keep his guard up. Earth had become a hotbed of foreign, extraterrestrial activity lately.

"The energy force is coming from that direction,"

Amara relayed to him.

As she spoke, a tall warehouse came into full view from the neighboring trees. It stood starkly gray in the deep night, but there were no lights visible. Still, he sensed a power source alien to his surroundings.

"I'm going inside," he told her.

Above him, Amara eased higher just a little, and he knew Amara kept her eyes on every move below.

He circled the warehouse once, seeing no guards, and then leapt to the rooftop. Among the exhaust pipes and ventilation shafts was a few broken antennas, but he detected no activity from them. He walked the perimeter and found an upper level window and made his way through it.

Inside the building was dark, but he could smell the circuitry, recently used, he knew. Most of the building's interior was archaic by Sundarian standards--the perfect place to hide off-world technology.

In the stillness of the dim interior he found what he was looking for. They were still in pieces, but on the ground floor of the warehouse was a crate of half-assembled communication beacons. He carefully examined them. Whoever was using the building had enough to make three, perhaps more. Too many, he thought. "Someone is coming, Elandrys," Amara's voice came through his communicator.

He set the beacon housing back in the crate and turned slowly, his vision scanning the dark forms. Mostly he saw crates and pallets, old shipping containers and bundles of cable.

And then the movement came, a lithe, svelte form that emerged from around a rack of stored metal.

Onyx burst from the racks of rods when she saw him.

"It's you!" she cried. "You were at that apartment where David was killed!"

Elandrys' watched her warily, not recognizing the curvy, purple–clad feminine form that rushed him. "Who are you?"

Onyx leaped and kicked straight for his head. He dodged and pivoted as she landed. She barely touched down then she spun backwards and sent a wicked heel in a quick snap to his neck. It grazed his shoulder as he evaded and caught her ankle in his grasp.

With a grunt, she wrenched her foot free and slammed her fist to his face. "Murderer! You killed a man and I'm bringing you to justice!"

He deflected her fist with a high block to her forearm and stepped back. "What? No! Wait! Stop!"

She turned and jabbed a mid-body kick to his hip.

"Sorry, but you brought this on yourself!"

He spun out of her leg's reach and backed up again as she charged him with chest-high kicks, none of which landed, but would have cracked a normal human's sternum.

"Why are--?"

Before he could finish the question, she spun into a fury of attacks that he blocked and deflected. Her speed was fueled by anger and emotional pain, her face below the mask set in clenched teeth and hissing.

He finally caught her forearm and held it high above them, making her stand on tiptoe, her other arm still flailing at him.

"All I have gotten on this planet is attacked," he said in a controlled voice as she wrestled against his hold. He released her arm and pushed her away. "Is that all you do here is attack and fight each other?"

"No, and we try not to kill each other, too," she bit out before lunging at him again.

Suddenly a bright light flashed for a second out one of the broken windows. Onyx paused her fighting, glancing at the large, sleek spaceship that gracefully set down in the weedy parking lot behind the warehouse. No sooner than the ship had touched than it seemed to shimmer and rematerialize as a woman. She nearly forgot her fight with the strange man she had seen in David's apartment. Before she could wonder more, the sound of the buildings pedestrian door opening was heard.

Amara entered from around the racks, drawing their attention away from their fight.

"Stop!" she commanded. "You must stop fighting! This is getting us nowhere."

Onyx backed away from Elandrys, eyes widening on the woman cloaked in blues, lavender, and gray who stepped closer to them.

"Where did you come from...I mean, how did you do that?" She chanced a quick look to the window to see that there was no spaceship outside. "Who are you?" she asked the mysterious woman now standing at the man's side. "What are you?"

"I am Amara," the woman said in a non-threatening tone. "This is Elandrys. We are not from this planet. We only came here searching for someone."

Onyx shook her head, still unable to believe her eyes. "Who?" Elandrys' posture relaxed. "I was following the energy trail before you attacked me. I believe we are after the same people."

Onyx shook her head. "People..." Too many odd things were happening too quickly. "What people?"

"Toroks," he said. "They were at your apartment before you and I arrived."

She still didn't understand. "Who are Toroks?"

"They are planet marauders," he said, "who take the natural resources from a planet, and often obliterate that planet afterwards."

A nervous laugh escaped her. "Wait... What? You're kidding, right?"

"No." Elandrys looked around at the warehouse and took a few steps past the row of racks. Now he spied the consoles at the far end. He immediately recognized them.

"This looks like their technology. They attacked my planet," he said, turning back to Onyx, "but we did manage to defeat them. Some must have fled here to Earth. Amara picked an energy signal. We have been following it."

Onyx slowly began to understand the situation. "That's why I saw you at the apartment." He nodded. "There were burn traces on the body."

"I do not have any other leads," she said as helplessness crept into her voice. "I have nothing else to go on. The police and FBI tell me it's classified." Another thought occurred to her. "Let me help you find them."

He shook his head without hesitation. "No, they are too dangerous. You must seek help from your police authorities. Warn them about a possible invasion."

Anger flashed back into Onyx with the hurt of losing her love. "They killed a friend of mine."

"Maybe she can help us," Amara said to Elandrys. "The Toroks are vicious. We do not know for sure how many there are here."

"Look, I am sorry. I really am," he said to Onyx before turning to Amara. "I do not want any more people to get hurt or even killed." He looked to Onyx, seeing the turmoil of emotions in her eyes. "We are only searching to see why one of my kind is here. We have Sundarian technology to do that."

Amara estimated Onyx. "She knows this planet. She can at least guide us." She looked up at the Sundarian. "We don't know this planet. If we work together, we may have a better chance of stopping the Toroks." Onyx nodded hopefully.

For a long moment he considered this, and then finally nodded. "Yes," he said reluctantly to Onyx. "We could possibly use your help if you are willing to face a dangerous task."

Onyx nodded. He pulled out his tracker. "We are following this signal. This way."

CHAPTER NINE

For a long time, Elandrys, Amara, and Onyx followed the tracker's signal. It led them deeper and deeper into the warehouse and eventually to a staircase accessing the underground chambers. The basement of the warehouse was dark and the staircase narrow, and the three of them descended into its depths.

Elandrys watched the steady flash of small light on the tracker. The signal beckoned them on to its target far below them. The staircase opened into a room dimly lit with caged light bulbs casting a little glow. It was empty except for discarded boxes and broken pallets. They moved on, following the tracker.

Across the room, another corridor opened, and this led to a series of hallways and corridors, all snaking below the warehouse in a labyrinth of darkness. The doors in the hallways they came across were all locked, and Elandrys saw no activity behind those locks on his tracker.

"How much farther?" Onyx asked.

Elandrys stopped, reading the tracker's signal. They were close. "There should be," he began, putting his hand to the door to their right, "something here. I'm picking up an energy source. It's pulsating, like a heartbeat."

Amara and Onyx stayed close behind him as he turned the door latch and opened the door slowly. Inside the beeping of instruments was heard.

Elandrys pushed the door wide.

Before them spread a series of consoles and tables. All of the tabletops were lit by small lamps that shown scant light on large sketches rolled out before them. They stepped closer, gradually realizing at what they were looking.

Large sheets of paper with gridlines formed the city above. The blueprints were marked in red highlighter pen for utility and government buildings and in green for waterworks and fuel sources. Escape routes out of the city in all four directions were circled in yellow.

Elandrys placed his tracker on the table, although it is bleeping a great deal.

Amara stood at Elandrys' side and glanced at the blueprints as he held up a sheet. Immediately, she knew what the plans outlined and what they could mean for Earth and its inhabitants. "No. This can't be."

He nodded as his grave expression settled on Onyx. "Your people will die if we cannot stop them. The Toroks will destroy this planet."

Onyx stepped closer, confusion leasing her face.

"They want something on this planet," Amara said, translating the prints into more helpful terms for Onyx. "This was done by someone who knows Earth and this city. The Toroks want something, and it looks like it's an energy source."

Elandrys placed the blueprints back on the table as they had been. "Let's see what else they have."

They moved quickly, noiselessly, into the next room. It was mostly storage, with metal racks crowding the view for more than a few feet. On the racks hung assorted supplies, mostly cables and cords. Overhead, boxes were stacked nearly to the ceiling.

"But that's all they want?" Onyx asked hopefully. "Energy?"

"Maybe more," he said. "We need to find them fast and stop whatever plans they have. Remember, communications first."

The floor beneath their feet swept downward, ever deeper beneath the warehouse, as they went to the next room.

"We have to stop them from communicating with their home planet," Elandrys said.

A muffled cry sounded from further in the room, past the rows of racks lined nearly wall to wall.

Onyx stopped, eyes widening at the soft cry. "Did you hear that?"

Again the low whimpering came to them, this time weak, sounding young and helpless.

Elandrys hurried through the racks with Amara and Onyx right behind.

Beyond the racks, an open space was blocked off by large plastic sheets. A muted light shone behind the sheets, casting an eerie silhouette on the plastic -- the image of someone lying on a table.

Amara rushed forward, warily, but desperate. She pulled the sheet back and nearly gasped. "Look!"

Elandrys was at her side in a second.

On the table lay a Sundarian girl, who appeared as a young Sundarian teen. She was strapped to the table surface and clad in only a smock. Her hair was limp and faded in color, and her face was ashen. From each of her arms ran long tubes to a panel of instruments behind her. Several lights blinked steadily as the tubes drew the girl's life force from her, draining her natural reserves, and seeping life from her.

Her eyes fluttered open, nearly unseeing.

Onyx stopped beside Amara. She put a hand over her mouth, feeling ill at the sight of the girl.

Elandrys steeled his emotions at the girl's plight. "I thought there was a Sundarian here."

At his voice, the girl opened her eyes wider, barely registering on them.

"That is horrible," Onyx said, still unsure of the magnitude of what was happening to the girl on the table. Obviously, this victim was having her life siphoned away, but she could hardly fathom who had such technology. "How can they do this?"

The Sundarian girl's unique anatomical structure was nearly fused with the machines in the building, running the Toroks' operation and powering their weapons. Elandrys stepped to the machines and examined the controls. The girl tried to reach for him, but her restraints held her down, not letting her fingers touch him.

Amara put a consoling hand to the girl's arm. "They are draining her energy. She's barely alive."

Elandrys carefully unplugged the life-draining tubes from where they connected the girl to the machinery. Amara deftly unfastened the restraints. The girl's eyes got large as she looked at him. He helped her sit up.

She leaned limply to him, weak from her confinement.

"It's all right," he said as she sagged against his chest. "I am a Sundarian, too. You are safe now. What is your name?"

She lifted her head to see him better. "Tess." She took a deep breath, slowly regaining her strength now that it was no longer being sucked out of her. Like Elandrys, her body had remarkable resilience, which was why the Toroks knew to keep her very weak.

Amara stroked Tess' arm. "You'll be okay with us."

Tess nodded. "I was taken while we were still fighting the Toroks on Sundaria -- me and others -- but they died on the ship. We crashed here." She took a deep breath, focusing more closely on Elandrys. "There are two Toroks and there are humans with them. They want--"

"Others are coming. "Amara's attention snapped to the racks. From far deep in the descending passages, footsteps raced.

Onyx faced the direction they had just come, the racks hiding her view of anyone entering the room. The footsteps neared quickly.

Elandrys pulled the girl from the table, keeping her upright as he prepared to battle whoever stepped from behind the racks. Tess leaned to him, fear in her face.

With a crash, Demolisher, Mystic, Kelvar, Zevyn, Polar, and Wraith Blade appeared from behind a falling rack. Cables and metal parts dashed to the floor, making a horrendous noise.

Tess whimpered at the sight of them.

Mystic stepped forward. "Who are you?"

Zevyn chuckled. "Another Sundarian, here on Earth. How did he find us?"

Kelvar nodded to Amara. "That one must have tracked us." He smiled slyly. "The girl's energy. It powers our weapons."

Elandrys pushed Tess behind him into Onyx's waiting arms. "You kidnapped a Sundarian child! If you have hurt her. . ."

Zevyn cautiously stepped further to one side, grinning maniacally. "Some of the spoils of war from your planet. We come to conquer and destroy. She serves our purpose." He smiled wider as Onyx tried to hide Tess behind her. "We do whatever it takes to get the job done. You should know that, Sundarian." He glanced now to Elandrys, his smile dropping. "Nothing stands in our way. The girl was taken as our hostage until we can find a way to defeat you and your wretched people."

Elandrys' hands balled into fists.

Zevyn's lip curled in a wicked grin. "She is nearly dead. You can have her then."

Tess sniffled at the comment and Onyx backed them away from the standoff forming.

Elandrys felt Amara step to his side as his eyes went to the second Torok. "What do you want with this planet?"

"The same thing we want from every planet. Even yours," Kelvar said, his voice rising as his eyes flashed. "Domination! You think you can stop us, Sundarian? This time you will die. Then we will return to Sundaria and end their existence!"

"You're fools," Elandrys bit out to the humans. "They will destroy the planet once they get what they want."

Wraith Blade laughed. "It doesn't matter," she said, whipping out both her blades. "Let them taste my blades!"

"Run, Onyx!" Elandrys shouted. "Take Tess with you, Amara, and get out!"

For a moment, Onyx stood frozen, watching as Wraith Blade expertly spun her blade and went into an attack against Elandrys. Amara didn't flee with Tess, but held her ground as Demolisher grabbed the girl's smock. Amara raised one hand, but it was smashed to the wall with one swipe of Demolisher's fist. She recoiled for a lunge, but Tess ducked and shoved her small shoulder into the large man's side. It was enough time for Amara to grab the girl and dodge out of the way as his fist plowed into the wall. The cement cracked and shuddered around the room.

"Run, Amara!" Elandrys called to her as he held off Blade Wraith's wakizashi.

Amara's grip on Tess tightened and they made their way through the fray.

Demolisher pivoted, flexing his fist as his targets ran from the room. He roared and unleashed a smashing fist into Elandrys' side. The Sundarian went down to one knee, narrowly escaping Wraith Blade's second blade point. Kelvar brought his powerful fist crashing across Elandrys' lower back, keeping him on one knee.

Elandrys got to his feet and unleashed a series of blows on Demolisher's side, cutting right under his arm as he missed a punch.

Suddenly Amara was at his side again, fighting right along with him.

It was all Onyx saw. She was trying to hold her own against Polar, Zevyn, and Mystic. She sidestepped a freezing hand Polar held up to her, only to find herself in Mystic's sights. She saw his mouth open and a word form at his lips, but didn't hear the word uttered. All she saw was a blinding light that sparked toward her.

Before she could drop, Zevyn's hand slammed into her face, knocking her out of Mystic's range. She fell to her knees, her vision swirling.

"What are you doing?" Mystic thundered. "I had her right where I wanted her!"

Zevyn raised his hand over the fallen woman as she scrambled, trying to move away. He stopped, glaring at his singed hand that had taken the brunt of Mystic's power. "What are *you* doing, Mystic? We're on the same side!"

Onyx shook her head, getting unsteadily to her feet as her temple throbbed.

Polar turned to face her.

Before she could react, his hand raised and an ice ray shot toward her. It hit her full in the chest, knocking her back against the wall, making her lose her breath.

"Chill out, girl!" he barked, laughing as she slumped to the wall.

She wheezed in a breath, feeling her lungs grow cold. She tried to move away, but Mystic stepped before him.

"Soma," he growled.

She tried to focus on him, but the whole room grew dizzily into a spin. The last thing she saw was Elandrys push Amara toward the doorway where Tess was peeking in.

"Amara," Elandrys said, his voice strained, "you must go and get help!"

Onyx tried to keep her eyes open, but the Sundarian was fading from her sight. She mouthed a word, but nothing came from her lips.

"I can't fight them alone," she heard Elandrys say.

Onyx couldn't believe they were losing -- these incredibly strong beings from another planet were losing, as was she.

"I can't leave you," Amara's voice came. "You need my help."

Onyx's eyes closed. Someone leaned over her. By the chill air, she knew it was the one called Polar.

"No," Elandrys said, sounding weaker. "Go and get help, Amara. Hurry!"

Onyx felt unconsciousness creep to her, but then a jolt went through her.

Across the room, Kelvar lowered his pulse weapon. He laughed as Onyx sat up, her nerves rattled, but fully awake.

"Can't have you sitting this one out, girl," he said with a snarl. "We might need you for something. You just stay right there."

The sting woke her senses, but made her movements lethargic. She looked to where she'd last seen Amara. The woman and Tess were gone.

"Stop her!" Zevyn ordered. "Don't let her get away!"

Amara raced down the hallway after Tess. The girl had regained her strength and was lightning fast at maneuvering the twisting corridors. She dared not call the girl's name, not wanting to give away their location.

The girl darted into the next hallway, out of sight. Amara followed, but when she got to the juncture of hallways, saw the girl nowhere. She looked into the right corridor and then the left. There was no sound.

"Tess," she whispered loudly, hoping the Toroks and the rest of Chaos wouldn't hear. "Tess!"

There was no answer.

Amara checked her bearings on her wrist locator, something was blocking her scanning of Sundarian energy. She had to get above ground and get help. It was the only way to help Elandrys and the rest of them. She couldn't spend time looking for the young Sund-arian girl.

"Tess!" she called as loudly as she dared.

In answer, a shard of ice whizzed past her arm. She turned to see Polar and Kelvar closing in quickly. She heard Kelvar charge his pulse cannon and knew that if he fired, she wouldn't be able to help anyone.

She ran around the next corner and took the stairs that led to the warehouse above. She climbed them swiftly and hurled open the door at the landing.

"Get her!" Polar bellowed.

A blast of cold air followed Amara as she dashed through the warehouse and into the dark parking lot outside.

"I'll bring help, Elandrys," she murmured, panting as she heard Polar and Kelvar closing in behind her. She raised her arms and leapt into the air, transforming into her ship self.

Only the Immortals could help them now.

Onyx was still stunned from her fight. She opened her eyes, trying to focus. Slowly, she realized she was in the warehouse underground, but now moved. A thick rope was wrapped around her chest, pinning her arms behind her as she leaned to the wall. She picked up her head that had topped forward to her chest. Fear suddenly swept over Onyx. "What did I get myself into?" Onyx thought to herself.

Beside her, the man -- or Sundarian -- she now knew as Elandrys was leaning to the wall, also tied up, and very awake. He glared at the Toroks opposite them.

Onyx's heart sank in her chest as she saw what he was watching. They were back in the warehouse above ground and the girl, Tess, was lying on a worktable, again strapped down. The tubes were back in both her arms, the machine draining her of life energy as she powered the console of instruments nearby.

Zevyn threw a broken cable against the wall. "Now we must hurry. Amara has gotten away." He spared a quick glance to where Onyx and Elandrys sat. "No doubt, she will most likely try to bring help." He looked to the girl on the table. "The FBI may still be planning an attack."

This got Wraith Blade's attention. She looked to each Torok. "How do you know them?"

Kelvar shrugged. "We saw them, their planet. Ordinary people with no major defenses. We were interested in the light energy that circled their planet." He nodded to Elandrys without looking at him. "We attacked the Sundarian's planet but were defeated."

Wraith Blade smiled. "Charming."

Kelvar didn't let the comment bother him. "One battle lost does not lose a war."

"And we will defeat you again," Elandrys said.

"Strong talk for a man tied up in an abandoned warehouse," Wraith Blade said with a giggle.

"We have conquered many galaxies and will not stop until we are the total domination of all," Zevyn said. "Our race is powerful, Mystic," he added, looking to where the large man was working on the instrument panel against another wall. "Unstoppable. By taming space, countless treasures, resources, and powers will be ours."

"Is that all you care about? Devastation and ruin?" Elandrys asked.

"Is there anything else, pathetic Sundarian?"

Mystic turned to look at them from his work. "I have established a strong signal. It seems that the high frequency transmitter is working, but needs more power to boost the signal for long range." He pointed at Elandrys. "And there's our answer."

Zevyn nodded. "Well, lucky us. We have to step up our time table. Amara will certainly be going for help."

"Going where?" Kelvar asked. "From whom? They know little about this planet, like we do."

"Do not underestimate Amara," Zevyn said. "She is very resourceful; they have gotten this far. She was there helping the Sundarians fight in the war, too."

Polar stood at the console beside Mystic, watching the screens. "I'll initiate the new protocols for the energy machine. The signal is working and all the computer viruses are in place. The ship is fully functional."

Kelvar gave a triumphant smile. "Then we are completely ready."

CHAPTER TEN

Amara's mind flew over the controls as she neared the Realm of the Immortals' perimeter. She had traveled as quickly as she could, knowing Elandrys and the Earth woman known as Onyx were losing their fight against incredible powers at the warehouse.

It was chancy to approach beings as omniscient as the Immortals, but it was necessary; she was desperate. There was nothing that the Immortals did not know, and she knew that they would be aware of Elandrys' dire situation.

Still, she had to ask -- had to plead for their help.

The ship entered the lighter atmosphere of the Realm of the Immortals. It was an outer layer of the planet's atmosphere, appearing as a city floating in a band around the solid below. Here the very air was pale golds and light blues, glowing lovely hues of brilliant energy, hinting of the gleaming Realm where the Immortals lived. Amara held her breath. She was always in awe of the Realm. It was a city surrounded by clouds and vigorous energy nearly tangible to the touch. She lowered to take the ship closer.

The dusty gold and pale blue air seemed to hold the ship with unseen fingers, as if to guide it gently to the layer where the Immortals resided. Soon the clouds parted enough to see the Realm.

Buildings three stories tall rose amid the blue and white of the sky and clouds. Terraces and bridges connected the tan stone buildings, most laced with green trees among twisting woody vines and braid-like trunks. The ornate stonework of the buildings was ancient, carved precisely by expert craftsmen. Delicate latticework crossed terrace rooms that overlooked the clouds and air passages.

Amara saw no one in these lofty rooms or on the building balconies now. She lowered into the immediate airways, watching for any sign of guards or messengers. There was no one. She knew the Immortals were aware of her entry. They always were. Nothing happened that they did not know or allow.

"Please go to the Counsel Building," a voice intoned from her communications.

Amara startled at first, but then nodded and addressed the communication center. "Thank you. I shall." Amara transformed into a woman. She walked towards the Counsel Hall.

The Counsel Hall stretched out before Amara several moments later. Its tall, brushed gold walls trimmed with coppery detailing rose around her, echoing with her footsteps as she approached the Counsel Room's double doors at the end of the hall. Around her, she could hear hushed voices of different languages, spoken by unseen beings from the corridors that branched out to either side.

She looked to one corridor, seeing no one, hearing only muted tones of beings beyond her sight. She had no time to puzzle over these murmurings now. Time was precious.

When she looked back to the double doors ahead of her, a tall, glowing, human-like figure blocked her way. He tilted his head, both curious and knowing at the same time.

"I must speak with the Immortals," she said as he stared at her.

He stepped to one side and gestured to the tall doors ahead, nodding to her.

She returned the nod and continued on.

The tall doors yawned open, and inside, Amara could see the ten thrones positioned in an arc around the galaxy on the floor tiling. The floor was deep lapis blue and dotted with pearly white circles of different sizes. One of those circles also had sapphire blue and malachite green shapes on it. She knew it represented Earth. On instinct, she glanced to another round shape of topaz gold and jade greens.

It was Sundaria, shining like a brilliant jewel in the heavens floor. Above her, a ceiling of blue sapphire and opalescent white and color towered over her, a representation of the universe in precious stones.

"Amara," said a deep male voice as she halted. "Welcome." The voice came from the center throne, from a male being seated in gold robes sitting at the middle arc throne. "Enter."

She bowed her head. "I am grateful you will see me."

"You are troubled," said a feminine voice from another throne.

Amara nodded to her. Around Amara, the ten thrones each held an Immortal, some female in form, others male. They were all draped in the flowing, luminous robes that shifted in color from gold to silver to blues and scarlet as they moved. Amara felt the weight of their collective knowledge and wisdom in the very air engulfing her.

She took a deep breath. "Toroks are on Earth and are planning an invasion."

"And you seek our help for this?" an Immortal said.

Amara turned to pinpoint him. "Yes."

"Why should we help earth?" another female said. "They are doomed to destroy themselves anyway. As for the Sundarian, sometimes a man meets his destiny on the road he took to avoid it."

Amara chose her words carefully as she addressed the Immortal female. "But doesn't everyone deserve a chance? There is some good still there on Earth. Please," she entreated, "you must find a way for me to help him. Earth will be another victim in the Toroks' path of devastation. Do not tell me you would stand by and do nothing."

"You are not an Earth woman," a thin male voice said. "Why do you care for them? Every planet, every universe, galaxy, every person, has their destiny, which they must fulfill. Earth has chosen its destiny, as we have foreseen in their future." His tone took on a haughty lilt. "It is appointed for every being to meet death. How they meet death is their choice."

She faced him. "People have fought to their last breath trying to stop the obliteration of the Toroks and you will not even help in fighting against them? You remain safe," she said, gesturing to the cobalt pillars and alabaster room around her, "safe inside these hidden walls."

He made a derisive snort. "Why would we give anyone's life so that one other can be saved and still have the same outcome?"

She shook her head. "What would you do if someone you loved could be saved? Would you stand by and watch as they met their demise? Or would you fight to save the person you loved? I know the Immortals are not as base as the barbaric beings that exist in the universe," she said, hearing a rift of murmurings around the arc. "I come to help save that which I love."

One of the female forms on a throne to her left sat straighter, making her robe glisten vibrant crimson. "Contrary to your belief of us," she said shrilly, "we are not without compassion. We will help you, Amara, but it will be solely on their choice and sacrifice."

Amara felt a great relief wash over her. "Thank you," she said quickly, smiling and bowing. "Thank you."

The center throne's figure raised his hand. "You will need help."

Before Amara could move or speak, he waved his fingers and a plume of crystal aurora borealis funneled between her and the center Immortal. It traveled around the arc, around Amara, and swept to the open arc side behind Amara. She turned to look as the glittery color dispersed and in its place stood two beings.

Several of the Immortals exchanged looks among themselves. Amara watched as the two new forms at the center of the arc's open side walked past her to the Immortals. One was male, with a powerful build and strong stride, his large hands balled in fists as if he was ready to do battle on the spot. A riveted metal harness was strapped over his wide shoulders and chest over his close-fitting gray suit. His black hair and beard were trimmed short, giving him a no-nonsense appearance. The other figure was female, slender but strong and agile, and wore only a bodysuit with a yellow and black torso with deep, dark red arms and leggings. Her hair was long and black. Her quick, dark eyes looked out from a spidery mask. Neither she nor the man glanced to Amara as they passed her and stood before the center Immortal's throne.

They both bowed curtly and stood tall, as if waiting orders.

"You have requested aid," the center Immortal said to Amara. He turned his head to indicate the two newcomers. "Your words have not fallen on deaf ears or hardened hearts."

The man and woman looked to Amara expectantly.

"Your help is needed," Amara said, uncertain how she should address them. "You have been chosen by the Immortals. The Toroks are on Earth and a Sundarian is there battling them. Will you help?"

The male looked at her curiously. "I am Gimel, Gimel Stone. I am from the colony planet Za'bal. I am an intergalactic bounty hunter." His eyes dropped over her, as if he could glean information from her by simply observing. "I was educated from a child in all forms of warfare, small arms weapons, and hand to hand combat." He nodded, seeming to estimate her. One of his hands opened and closed into a tight, hard fist again. "I can also speak many diverse languages. I would be glad to help crush some Toroks. I have seen what they can do to planets," he said, and then added in a dark tone, "and they must be stopped."

Amara nodded. "I would be grateful for your help, Gimel Stone."

The woman spoke. "I am Venus. I was born on my home planet, Raydoria Prime." She looked to the ceiling of constellations and galaxies painted on the tiles. "The people of Raydoria Prime are born with the strength," she said, now resting her attention back on Amara, "and energy of our Raydorian sun. I am also an elemental scientist." She nodded slowly. "I'm just sick of hearing about the

Torok and their path of destruction. But just us?" She looked from Amara to Gimel. "Don't we need more than just us two?"

"As the Immortals have already foreseen, there are just two Toroks on Earth," Amara explained. "They have captured a Sundarian and an Earth woman, as well as a little Sundarian child. Your skills are very much needed. Earth is surely in great peril."

The double doors at the end of the hall flung open. A large man in royal blue and yellow body armor entered. His face was covered with a fitted royal blue helmet that showed only his yellow eyes. He crossed the room quickly, seeming to grow larger with every step. He towered over Amara, sized her up, and then looked to the Immortals.

"I have overheard all this and I wish to go with them," he said in a guttural voice.

The middle Immortal shook his head slightly. "No, you are not ready for such a battle, Celestial."

"But you know I am," said Celestial, his hands closing into royal blue gauntleted fists. "I have been given a gift to use for others. What reason is there to have a gift such as mine and not use it for this very purpose?"

Amara felt precious time slipping away from her as Elandrys was fighting for his life and Earth. "The Toroks are plaguing the galaxies and other solar systems. We have to stop their killing of innocent beings," she reminded. "We must do something now. Please!"

The Immortals seemed to converse with each other without speaking and only barely moving. They leaned slightly to each side, nodding almost imperceptibly.

Finally, the center Immortal's gaze went to the four awaiting an answer. "You may go. You all may go," he said to Celestial. "This is your choice. And for the record, you all are right." He looked again to Amara. "For what it's worth, Amara, you all have made the choices we have foreseen."

He held his hand to the Immortal at his left. The second Immortal placed three small devices in his palm.

"These," the first Immortal said, standing and reaching out his hand to Amara, "will help Gimel Stone, Venus, and Celestial return to their home planets should they succeed in defeating the Toroks. You take exceptional warriors with you, Amara. Use them well."

She held the transporters close and bowed her head. "I am very grateful." She turned to her new comrades. "Quickly. We must leave now. I'll tell you more as we travel."

The heavenly ceiling suddenly split at the center and the tiling shifted to either side, showing the real sky above. The entire top of the room spread open.

"You may leave now," the Immortal said.

Amara immediately transformed into her spaceship form and hovered just feet off of the floor. They all stood in awe of Amara. "She has some secrets we must quickly learn about" Says Gimel.

They all looked in bewilderment at the transformed Amara hovering in the air.

"Please, we must hurry!" a pale illusion of Amara appeared in the hatch. Amara beckoned them inside.

With skilled practice, Gimel Stone, Venus, and Celestial each leaped into the air and through the opened hatch. *Amara* lifted into the sky and zipped out of sight.

"You are a ship and a woman?" asked Venus, "how is that possible?" Amara now in her illusion form is sitting behind the front console looking out the front port view.

Without looking back as they all took seats, "As I said, I will tell you as much as I possible can on the way."

The Immortals watched the ship swiftly disappear. The Immortal who had given Amara the transportation devices nodded with satisfaction as he watched the ceiling close again. "They all agreed without thought of themselves. Only for others."

The female Immortal to his left smiled. "We have chosen well."

CHAPTER ELEVEN

O nyx heard little of what was exchanged between the Toroks and Chaos. All she could really see was the hopelessness of the situation. She was in over her head, and she knew it. This was more than she was, more than new powers from an ancient stone and her makeshift attire when she created herself as Onyx. These beings -- the members of Chaos with their superhuman powers and strengths, and these otherworlders who could change form and could power devices with their bodies alone -- they were beyond her. Whatever that stone her parents had brought back had done to her, she was no match for these beings. Yes, she was much stronger, but she was outmatched when held up against these beings.

She chided herself, ignoring her cramped arms and numb fingers beneath the rope. At least she was better off than Tess.

The Sundarian girl lay on the table, semi-conscious as her body was drained of energy -- and spirit -- as she powered the equipment. As quickly as she had recovered before when Elandrys freed her, she now lapsed back into a state of near death. Her breathing was shallow, her chest barely moving as she exhaled, and her face was drawn of color again. Already her full lips were becoming dehydrated and her eyes fluttered as she struggled for life.

Onyx's heart broke watching her. "The girl doesn't look good at all," she said quietly to the Sundarian still bound beside her. As much as it hurt her to watch Tess suffer, she could not imagine what it was doing to Elandrys to see his fellow kind fight for her life.

But his voice was hopeful, something Onyx did not expect. "She will make it," he said. He shifted to see Onyx better. "It's no use struggling with those bands. They are unbreakable."

Onyx didn't feel like being looked at, especially by someone she had attacked. She kept her attention on Tess. "Maybe I bit off more than I can handle. I'm not a superhero type," she admitted, sighing beneath the tight ropes around her chest. "I just wanted to find David's killer."

He chuckled lowly, and she looked to him. "I am no hero either," he told her. "I just want to do what's right. I have only met you and you have taken on a foe that is sure to annihilate us both." When she shook her head, he said, "That's courage. Let it remain longer."

His words made her feel a little better, but still despairing. "Do you think Amara made it?" She glanced to the painted-over window to see a crack of light from outside, searching for a glimpse of the clever woman's return. "Will she come back with help?"

He nodded. "Amara will be here. She has never let me down and she will never leave me." His gaze took in the warehouse, from the supplies to the outer doors and windows to the hall doorways. Chaos and the Toroks weren't in sight. "The Toroks do not have their full armory or a full Torok force. We still have a chance of beating them."

Onyx frowned, looking around at the consoles and what she could see of the warehouse from where she sat beside the wall. She had little hope in beating the odds against them.

Deeper in the warehouse, the Toroks and Chaos were destroying everything that could be seen as evidence of their work there. They had already cleaned out the rooms they had used for storage and piled some of their equipment, old supplies, and unneeded resources in a few locations. Once they blew up the place, nothing would be recognizable. Every scrap of instrument, computer equipment, stolen supplies, and blueprints would be fully destroyed.

Mystic slung a roll of fiber optic cable onto the stack in the last room they were clearing. "Make sure nothing is left. We don't want anything linking this to us." Unlike the Toroks, he, Demolisher, Polar, and Wraith Blade couldn't hop planets. They still had to call Earth home, even if they each did have a massive grudge against the inhabitants. "Absolutely nothing."

Demolisher nodded to the Toroks who joined them from their work in another room. "This is it, the last pile of anything that shows we were here."

Wraith Blade stepped into the room, giving the pile a nod. "We're about done here." She handed Mystic, Demolisher, and Polar sets of earplugs. "Here, place these in your ears."

Kelvar watched the humans stick the rubbery sponges in their ear canals. "Hurry. We probably don't have much time."

With a long, satisfying study of the room, certain that they had thought of everything, they all left the room and headed back to the main console room. They had just a few loose ends to tie up.

Collectively, the Toroks and Chaos gave Tess on the table a glance, and then each looked to where Onyx and the Sundarian were still tied up against the wall.

Polar went to the consoles and checked the screens. His eyes lingered on one that showed the schematics for a warhead. A side panel ran a countdown. "All is ready with the transmission device. The warhead is ready to launch at our command."

The Toroks nodded in satisfaction.

"This will give Toria our location," Kelvar said. "It is encoded with information about Earth. Everything they need for total invasion -- their defense technology and communications."

Wraith Blade leaned one hip to the console and crossed her arms. She nodded to Elandrys and Onyx at the wall. "What about them and the girl?"

Zevyn gave them a dismissive look. "Leave them. The girl has served her purpose." He glanced at Tess who was weaving in and out of consciousness. "She is nearly dead anyway."

Elandrys had spent much of his bound time trying to rub the nylon ropes against a jagged block behind him, keeping his eyes on the doorway where sounds had come from further in the warehouse. For roughly half an hour, crashing and cursing had come from the interior of the building. He couldn't quite figure out what Chaos and the Toroks had been doing, but it sounded like they were searching for something or destroying something.

The nylon of the ropes resisted damage on the broken block behind him. He had been about to speak more to Onyx when Chaos and the Toroks came back into the room.

Elandrys now watched them speak among themselves, a few of them looking at him and Onyx; no one looked at Tess for more than a brief glimpse. They were draining her into an early death and she was no more than a living, flesh and blood battery to them.

Demolisher strode toward them, grinning maniacally. "All you softies will make a nice little fire when we're done here. Just like all the rest of these fragile little rats running around the city." His gaze hardened on Onyx. "Even you. I don't know who you think you are, but you're nothing more than a girl in a Halloween costume."

Onyx bristled at this, struggling against the ropes binding her as his cruel laugh rang off the walls.

"You have no idea what you walked into here." He shook his head. "You and your fancy outfit. You're just like all the rest -- a soft little pile of--"

Suddenly the building shook, cracking the cement floor and making the walls tremble.

A spaceship burst through the exterior wall, shoving her way nearly to the console, effectively wiping the grin from Demolisher's face as he gaped in astonishment.

Elandrys knew who had arrived, it is Amara. Everyone on their feet jumped out of the way as racks and boxes tumbled, sending debris and concrete dust in every direction. The ship cleared the area, pushing tables and a few chairs into the racks, bulldozing a wide path of dust. Gray dust swirled through the room as *Amara* burst the block wall. Amid the fine particles, Gimel Stone, Celestial, and Venus stepped out as Amara transformed into herself, all three armed to the teeth and ready to do battle.

Zevyn crouched, batting away the dust particles hazing around them, never taking his eyes from the new intruders. When he recognized their method of intrusion, his surprise was replaced by grim determination. "Amara came back sooner than I bargained for."

Polar gave them a swift estimation. "What's this?" He nodded at the three beings from the Realm of the Immortals. "Who are they?"

Amara ran to Elandrys and gave him a quick embrace, searching his face and form for injuries. "You're okay?" She hastily untied him and then turned to Onyx. "Are you hurt?" She threw off the ropes, looking back to Elandrys. "Can you fight?"

Elandrys leaped to his feet and pulled Onyx up with one hand as Amara stood. "We're ready." He estimated her traveling companions. "It looks like you brought company."

Venus flexed her hands as if itching to grip something, sizing up Chaos and the two Toroks. "I'm Venus. We are here to stop you."

Demolisher made a fist with each hand, eager for a showdown. "Are you now? Well, what are you waiting for? You can definitely try."

Zevyn nodded to Kelvar as the rest of Chaos positioned opposite Elandrys and his comrades. "Hurry! Start the transmission device!" He waved an arm at the countdown on the screen at the console. "Program the warheads and launch!"

Wraith Blade drew her swords, swinging them in easy loops before her as she snickered at Gimel Stone and Venus. The blades spun in an infinity fashion, forming two loops of lethal edges before her. "Three new trick ponies." She stopped the blades and pointed one wakizashi at Amara. "Is that it, Amara?"

Rather than answer, Amara sent her a toxic glare.

Polar looked at Celestial, judging the skin-tight armor the Baltorian wore. "So, who are you?"

"Your end to this madness." Celestial told him.

Polar chuckled, no amusement in his face. "Is that so?"

Elandrys stepped in front of Amara as Wraith Blade pointed at her with both sword tips. "You're not leaving here without a fight."

Wraith Blade laughed. "Come, then. Death awaits you!"

The room erupted in a fight, with Chaos and the Toroks siding against Elandrys and the team Amara had brought back. Amara slipped back as Polar sent a ice blast her way. She dodged it and got to the table where Tess lay helpless. The girl's face was turned toward the battles, but her eyes were barely open. Amara quickly unfastened the straps and lifted the girl up.

Behind her, Zevyn threw an incendiary bomb at Venus, nearly branding her and Celestial and Gimel Stone. The last man stepped before them and raised his wrist, creating a force field the blocked the bomb blast. It deflected and zipped up to a wall, making a scorching hole there. He pulled a small fire bomb from his harness, adroitly flicked it open into a boomerang, and then slung it at the Torok.

Zevyn dodged it and it circled back to Gimel Stone, who caught it in one large hand. A sudden whooshing sound made them all look to the wall above, just below the high ceiling. Zevyn's fire bomb had set off more fires along the wall and ceiling, where the flames spread as storage boxes caught fire.

Tess pulled herself from Amara and tried to go to Elandrys' aid, but Amara grabbed her hand. "No, come," she told the girl. "I must get you to a safe place!"

They ducked out of sight behind a mound of fallen racks just as Kelvar charged his pulse gun. He got off one shot at them, but Zevyn waved him off.

"Get the launches underway!" Zevyn shouted over the noise of the fire and pairs of fighters. "This console is going to short-circuit! Get to the second controller!"

Kelvar nodded and raced down the back hallway as Zevyn turned to face his next fight.

Elandrys ran after Kelvar. The hallway was filling with smoke, making following difficult, but he could hear the Torok cough every few feet. The smoke thinned after a few turns of the hallway and Elandrys stopped when he saw Kelvar in a small room he nearly ran past. The Torok stood at a console with very few controls, nothing like the former room's consoles with numerous buttons and gauges.

Kelvar turned as Elandrys ran at him. Kelvar raised his pulse cannon, but the space was too tight and the Sundarian was on him instantly. Elandrys sent a smashing fist into the Torok's face, making him crash back into the console.

"You have learned nothing from your defeat on Sundaria!" he shouted.

Kelvar rammed the cannon across the Sundarian's face, but Elandrys stepped back out of reach. "You have learned nothing about Toroks!"

Elandrys sidestepped the next swing of the cannon. "Why do you seek the suffering and killing of others?"

A glint came to the Torok's eyes. "I seek conquest! Make no mistake about that, Sundarian!"

Elandrys punched him in the jaw. "You will not have it today or as long as I live!"

Kelvar's head snapped back and he grunted heavily from the punch. He laughed as blood seeped to his chin. He ducked the next punch to his face. "I can arrange for your death now!"

He lunged for the controls again, this time reaching the red button that was flashing.

A whistling noise rose as Kelvar's hand mashed the button and enabled the launch. He turned to face Elandrys, whose eyes were on the small panel where a green sequence was now blinking a coded location of the warheads engaging in their deadly mission.

Kelvar watched the dismay cover Elandrys' face. "So it's true," he said, enjoying the moment. "You Sundarians are relentless, but so are we. You will never stop us."

"We will stop you," Elandrys said, turning to him. "Just as we have done before."

"See this, Sundarian?" Kelvar said, nodding at the countdown that was quickly flicking numbers. "It's over. We win."

Elandrys stared at the panel, knowing it was true, and that there was nothing he could do about it. As much as he hated it, the Torok's words were true. He turned and attacked Kelvar. He shoved him against the wall, but his thoughts overtook what his muscles were doing to the Torok.

He slammed a fist into Kelvar's chest. *I've failed this unsuspecting planet,* he thought. *I know it's going to end in a war to the absolute death of everyone here.*

He pounded a fist into the Torok's stomach as his target nearly fell.

I cannot just halt the Toroks, he knew. *I have to extinguish them.* The hunters in the forest came to his mind. Even though they were killers of animals, they were not killers of their fellow human. Even they were nobler that these Toroks who were determined to see the wholesale slaughter of mankind. *Will I see millions enslaved or die?*

He raised a fist for another beating to Kelvar's already bloodied face. His knuckles made impact, bringing another spurt of Torok blood and tissue.

I have defeated them before, Elandrys knew. *My people have defeated them. I will defeat them again. I will overcome again.*

He cocked his arm back for another onslaught, but the Torok sagged in his grip, unconscious and limp. Elandrys let him fall.

Amara pulled Tess close as they hid behind the fallen racks. The girl was quickly gaining strength now that she wasn't hooked up to the tubes siphoning off her life.

"She's so strong," Tess murmured, her dark eyes following Wraith Blade's fluid movements as she and Mystic fought Gimel Stone.

Nearby, Onyx was trying to help, but spent much time staying out of Celestial's insanely long reach. Even one hit by the massive blue and yellow armored man would clearly damage her. Celestial was holding his own against Polar and Demolisher, but there were no clear winners yet.

Amara looked to the doorway where Elandrys had chased after Kelvar. The other Torok had crouched behind the console where the countdown was flashing -- the counter was stuck or malfunction-ing. Amara couldn't tell which.

"But she has no honor," Amara said in a low tone as she watched Wraith Blade before looking back to the console.

"No. None," Tess agreed.

Wraith Blade's style had changed. The glee she had in the fight was gone, and now something else took its place. Her sword blades flashed in the smoky air, seeming to cut the dust into slivers. Her movements were powered by pain, by regret, not her usual training and finesse. To anyone watching, she looked like a ruthless huntress, hitting her target -- Gimel Stone -- as he blocked her assault. But her face held hurt, a wounded soul, painful memories that drove her movements. Beneath her chest beat the heart of a woman far colder than anything even Polar could manage.

Gimel Stone had lost few battles, and now, as he fought off his very skilled enemies, both the dangerous edges of Wraith Blade and the corrupted magic of Mystic, he saw only part of the fight raging. He didn't know -- couldn't have known -- that the man behind the magic was also warring with himself. It didn't show in Mystic's face; that loss, a loss of such magnitude that it had split him in two, didn't show in his features. Instead, his expression of steely determination was locked as he threw powerful spells at Gimel Stone. Mystic was now two forces; the changed man who would use every trick and cunning maneuver he knew, and also the man who had lost all, leaving only callousness and revenge.

Amara could see some of the driving force in the members of Chaos as they fought, but not all of it. She did, however, see the change in vengeance in these powerful enemies who struck back at not new foes, but at themselves.

Tess' head lifted from her crouch. Her eyes opened wider. "Do you hear that?"

Amara nodded as she singled out the faint whistle coming from the doorway. Her attention snapped to the console. Even from the distance, she could now see through the dust a square button with the words "ENGAGED" flash.

Tess darted from her, running through the smoke and battles and falling cinders.

Amara dashed after her. "Tess! What are you doing?"

Tess didn't stop. "We have to stop a bomb!"

Amara grabbed her shoulder as they reached the console. "What? A *bomb*?"

Tess pointed to the fighting, indicating no one in particular. "I heard them talking! They're launching a bomb to hit the nuclear reactor plant!"

Amara instantly knew. "That's where Elandrys chased the Torok... They've initiated the sequence from another location." She shook her head, focusing on Tess. "I don't have any weapons to stop a bomb!"

Tess leaned to the console as a wave of weakness grabbed her. "We can take the Torok weapon." Her eyes found the screen showing the bomb now engaged and on its way to destruction. She tapped the screen. "Here's the trajectory," she said. She dropped to her knees and felt around inside the console until she pulled out a pulse cannon. She leapt to her feet and held up the weapon. "They always kept one stashed there." She nodded quickly, looking to Amara. "Can we reach the target?"

Amara took her hand and pulled her with her through the battles of the smoke filled room, eluding a burning rack as it fell.

"We're going to try," she said once they were outside. She raised her arms to transform. "We're going to try, Tess!"

CHAPTER TWELVE

The city of Lexington Park came slowly back to life as dawn stretched across the streets. Shadows dissolved, shrinking back against buildings as the sun climbed into the smoky skies. Stores opened and children emerged from homes with parents, sitters, nannies, and grandparents in tow, ready for a day of parks, zoos, play, and day camp.

To the city, the day was as any other, warm and sunny, with the smells of street vendors competing with traffic fumes and construction dust. For most, it was a day of work and play, arguments and triumphs, crime and accomplishment, romance and heartbreak.

The streets were full of cars, bikes, and pedestrians caught between the tall buildings and trees. Few noticed the spaceship *Amara* fly overhead, and most dismissed the shadow passing over the streets as a stray cloud.

But *Amara* and Tess, now sitting at the wide port window at the front of the craft, were searching, hoping to find the result of the Toroks' plans before the warhead could find its target.

Tess sat eagerly forward in the craft, her fingers nervously twisting the necklace at her throat, the pulse cannon lying across her knees. Her frenzied system was still recovering from fueling the Toroks' instruments and what little nourishment she had had during her time of confinement. Her brown eyes moved over the foreign city below, seeing the people moving busily about their morning. She was still rattled by her ordeal, but now her emotions were frayed for the humans below who knew nothing of the plots against them.

Her gaze traveled over the streets, stopping at the large gray stone library, the community center, the schools and playgrounds, the shops and small factories.

"I'll head to the other side of the city and make a sweep back around," *Amara* said from the nearest speaker to Tess. "Look for a smoke, fire, or electrical particle trail."

Tess nodded, searching the streets below. "Will it be the...?" She pointed as a thin cloud of white smoke flared from their left. "Look, Amara! There's the bomb now!"

The warhead became more defined as it advanced, its smoke trail becoming slenderer as it passed.

"Engaged!" *Amara* directed.

Amara engines burst to life, moving her forward at a incredible momentum towards the bomb.

Tess picked up the Toroks pulse cannon. Tess found and wore a special set of vision goggles that helped see the bomb trail in the bright daylight, but every little tilt of her head redirected her target.

Amara opened her hatch door and Tess positioned herself to fire the Torok Pulse cannon at the warhead.

The screen in the lens before her left eye in the goggles showed the green lines of the city below with the red needle-like warhead moving away toward a square building ahead. Beside it were two large columns whose bases widened at the ground.

At first, she thought they were water towers, but then a white LED on the screen blinked.

NUCLEAR REACTOR.

She gasped, and then pushed two buttons to her right of the pulse cannon. A blue line pulse blast raced out from *Amara's* hatch door and followed the red needle on her goggle lens. The blue line was her target recognition, but as it caught up with the red needle warhead, it veered off to the left.

"I missed," she groaned, sinking back in her chair. She flipped off the goggles and stood up.

Out the window, she saw the bomb closing in on the reactor plant. Amara closed the hatch door.

"We can't reach it in time," *Amara* said. "Please sit back down, Tess. This may get very rough."

Tess slowly returned to the chair, her eyes fastened on the speeding bomb ahead. "I failed, Amara."

The warhead struck the plant's core, making the building fold in on itself. The blocks crumbled, sending up a plume of smoke and dust.

But there was no explosion.

Tess dashed to the side window as *Amara* turned back to avoid the debris thrown into the air from the impact. Out the window, she could see the reactor plant falling away.

"There was no explosion," *Amara* said, her voice confused.

"It was a warhead," Tess said. A sudden ringing began in her ears, and then a high-pitched shriek filled the compartment. She grabbed the chair back as she made her way back to the front of the ship.

"...and sit down," came *Amara's* voice through the squeal trapped in Tess' head.

"What is that?" Tess pushed her hands over her ears as she dropped into the chair. She closed her eyes, trying to block out the screaming sound. "What kind of bomb is that?"

"No, that was a sound transponder," *Amara* replied. "They are using the power of the nuclear reactor to heighten the sound waves."

There was a pause, and then she asked curiously, "Why would they do that?"

"The sound is killing me." Tess could barely hear her. A flashing light to her left chair screen grabbed her attention, even with her eyes nearly shut. The screen stopped flashing, and then words appeared.

"I know you are having difficulty hearing me, Tess," *Amara* wrote on the screen in Sundarian characters. "I'm shutting down the outside air ventilation. It will get warm in here, but it will block out some of the sound and you will be able to hear better."

"O-Okay," Tess said, nodding. She slowly took one hand away from her ear. The high squeal was still there, but not as deafening as before.

"Is this any better?" *Amara* asked.

Tess sighed and nodded. "Thank you, Amara."

The Sundarian writing on the screen vanished. Already, Tess could feel the air warming without the proper ventilation.

"We have to stop this," *Amara* said. The ship slowly turned to circle the reactor plant.

Tess nodded, watching the display screen now showing a series of numbers and maps flash.

"I am scanning for a power source," *Amara* said. "If we can get to that and disable it, which may work to stop the sound waves."

Tess found the goggles she had used to shoot at the bomb and put them back on. In her left eye's screen, she could see back images of the reactor plant. For a moment, the collapse of the main building froze onscreen. In it, she could see people running from the building.

She couldn't bare it. She took off the goggles and looked out the window. They were close enough to the plant again to see people in the parking lot and around the tall towers. All had their hands clamped over their ears in anguish, some running wildly, others slumping to their knees or squirming in the fetal position as they lay on the pavement. People from the reactor and the buildings around were all swarming madly, running, falling, and screaming.

The city below was in chaos now. It was no longer orderly traffic and pedestrians on the street. Now, the shrilling screech had reached the city and everyone was feeling the maddening sound.

Most people were on the ground, writhing in pain from the shrieking sound. Cars had crashed, blocking streets. Two trains had derailed near a parking lot and the station, sending clouds of smoke and debris in every direction. The second half of one train had smashed into an apartment building and two high rises. The buildings were in stages of falling, leaning, and dumping their people from windows and balconies. In some buildings, the windows had shattered. The tone set off every siren, making squad cars, ambulances, security alarms, and firehouse bells add into the screaming crescendo no one could escape.

The sound waves from the reactor impact swelled out, shattering and ripping eardrums and blood vessels across the city. *Amara* dove lower, looking for a good place to land.

Tess could see the looks on peoples' faces as they descended. It was ghastly, with men and women with blood streaking from their noses, mouths, and ears, and some tearing at their eyes with their fingers. Cars were smashed into buildings. Twisted metal from the train collisions had bowed out from residual impacts along guardrails. Everywhere people were screaming and running in confused circles or falling to their knees.

Tess' hand dropped from her other ear, gaping at the destruction. The city was in total chaos.

Amara hovered over the parking lot that was now overrun with screaming people and broken metal. "We must help them, Tess."

Tess nodded, and braced herself for the unrelenting noise. "I'm ready."

Amara landed in the parking lot of the reactor plant and told Tess she would transform and help her. The area was like a war zone, with people screaming and holding their temples as blood dripped from their ears and noses. Portions of the building had fallen, trapping people and workers beneath, some dead and others dying or maimed for life. Humans were not equipped to lift the fallen walls from the writhing forms beneath, but they were trying. Those who could function with the sound filling their heads were using everything they could find to use as levers to help their trapped friends and coworkers. Several men were leaning on a long metal pole to lift a wall off a woman whose legs were crushed. As soon as she could move away, she desperately crawled out from the slab of wall on top her. The men let the wall drop and one of them helped the woman up, nearly carrying her at his side as he hurried them to the parking lot.

Tess watched the men and woman, her eyes searching out other humans helping each other. Most were too incapacitated to help anyone else.

"They cannot protect themselves from the Toroks," she said lowly as she readied to leave *Amara*. She had stuffed her ears with small pieces of cloth, as *Amara* had directed when they were landing, but it did little to lessen the screeching sound. She shook her head as *Amara* signaled her transformation.

"Go! Get to the power source!" *Amara* told her. "Hurry!"

"Yes!" Tess nodded and stood at the hatch as *Amara* opened the entry. As soon as it dropped, she leaped out. She ran off toward the somewhat intact entrance of the building where smoke was bellowing out.

Amara transformed into her flesh form and quickly followed. She fought her way through the throng of people running pell-mell and collapsing on the asphalt. One man dropped nearly in front of her, holding his hands to his ears as his mouth foamed a bloody froth. She knelt and made him face her. At first, he shook and tried to pull from her hands on his shoulders, but her grip tightened and she made him face her again.

"I'm going to help you," she told him.

His eyes rolled in his head, unfocused on her.

She ripped off his uniform sleeve, noting he was a plant worker, likely a janitorial staff rank judging from his name patch and clearance tags. She tore smaller pieces from the sleeve. "This will help some," she said, gently rolling and tucking a small patch of material into his ear to act as a plug against the sound. She did the same with his other ear. "Leave those in."

He nodded, eyes squeezed shut as he panted. "It's madness... It's unlike...any, anything I've ever seen," he wheezed.

"This is all we can do right now," she said, standing up. "Rest until you can stand and then get away to safety."

179

She moved to another couple, two women in hazmat suits minus the hoods, who were watching her through bloodshot eyes. They were leaning on each other, their suits reddened with blood from their ears. Both were breathing hard and coughing. Amara repeated the process as with the man, this time using the small pockets of the women's suits. Immediately the women calmed, shaking still, but now understanding that Amara was trying to lend them aid.

"What is it?" one woman asked, searching Amara's face for hope. "No one can stand up. It's crazy!"

Amara helped them to sit against each other at the parking lot curb. "It's an equilibrium imbalance. As soon as you can balance, get to medical attention."

The other woman turned her head and vomited.

Amara stood and looked around. All across the lot, people were falling to their knees and rolling into tucked positions, holding their ears, retching. A few workers had witnessed her treatment and were now ripping cuffs and sleeves from their clothes to stop up in their ears. Coworkers were helping those who were already unable to properly function from nausea or dizziness. As fragile as these humans were, Amara decided, they were trying to overcome the noise and help each other.

She turned to look at the building belching smoke and dust. The noise wasn't quite as acute for her, but these humans -- and Sundarians -- were highly affected. She raced in to find Tess.

The shrilling sound had reached the warehouse across the city. It exploded through the air, penetrating the thick block walls, hitting every ear inside. The auditory attack had little impact on Chaos and the Toroks, as they were equipped with earplugs.

Inside, Celestial suddenly stepped back from his fight with Demolisher and grabbed his ears as the unrelenting sound assaulted the building. He clenched his teeth as the shriek permeated the walls and rattled the windows and racks.

Demolisher chuckled, tapping the side of his head. "Not ready for the blast?" He roared a laugh as Celestial cringed from the noise. "You come here with your mighty ideas and mission, ready for battle, and a little noise bothers you?"

Celestial shook his head, trying to empty his ears of the sound, but could not.

"These Immortals," Demolisher nearly spat. "They send a boy to help! A boy and a woman!" He advanced on Celestial. "This isn't even your fight. What do you know of this planet?"

Celestial stood straighter, but the noise was starting to disorient him. "I know they're prey to the Toroks. That is enough."

"Is it? Why?" Demolisher shook his head, grinning at the large being in snug armor now beginning to cringe with nausea. He watched with a mixture of curiosity and condescending amusement.

"You think all these millions of little worms of human beings on this planet are worth your life? They're worth nothing. I know this. I've lived among them. This green and blue orb you're on is no different than any other rock circling any other star. They're driven by the same thing that drives the Toroks."

Celestial steadied his stance, trying to understand the large man before him through the noise. "Greed drives the Toroks. Greed for power, for control."

Demolisher stopped grinning and a different sort of lethal smile overtook his face. "Exactly." Every muscle in his body stiffened as he stood to his full height, his hands balling into fists of emotional tension. "Greed. And what did that get me?"

Celestial didn't understand, but before he could ask, Demolisher continued.

"Isolation? It was supposed to get me money!" He threw a punch at Celestial, who dodged. Demolisher pulled his fist from the cracked wall block. "I was going to sell that uranium and get filthy rich! Now look at me!" He rotated, following the Baltorian as he moved around him, holding one hand at his ear. Demolisher's eyes narrowed on the armored being as years of misguided fury found a new direction. "This," he said, holding up his large fist as dust fell from his ultra-strengthened skin, "this is what I got. Nearly limitless might, but no money. No real human contact. No family, no one else like me. I lost my girlfriend when I was bestowed this *flesh*. I lost everything else!"

He slammed a fist into Celestial, a full force punch that landed, but was blocked by his raised forearm. The blue and yellow armor deflected the blow, sending Demolisher off balance. Celestial pivoted, keeping on his feet despite the wave of equilibrium sloshing through his brain. He felt his armor slowly begin to fade at his left arm as his concentration weakened. He tried to muster the strength and focus to keep it intact.

"And you come down here with your fancy armor and lofty ideas," Demolisher scoffed, smashing his fist into Celestial's shoulder as the armor dissipated from that spot. Seeing the weakened opening, he grinned and sent a double-punch to the shoulder.

Celestial fell to one knee. The noise was so bad in his head that he could barely stay conscious. His armor began fading in numerous spots on his body. Above the noise, he could see Demolisher also in pain, but a different type of pain. He had never so vividly seen emotional torment as he did now.

He staggered back to both feet, evading Demolisher's next punch that was driven by years of lonesomeness -- he had tasted that solitude himself, even while surrounded by well-meaning Eminent Counselors, his surrogate family. "I understand being alien in a world unlike me," he said, his voice drowned out by the noise. He knew Demolisher had heard him by the irate look crossing the uranium-strong man's face. "I know being an orphan, even among others like me."

"What's this? Some kind of off-world psychology?" Demolisher's lip snarled into a cutting feature on his face. "You think you know me mechanical boy?"

"I am not a mechanical boy," Celestial said, fighting to remain upright. "I am tissue and fiber, blood and pain, just as you."

"You know nothing of me!" Demolisher sent a crushing blow to Celestial's chest as the silvery blue armor there faded. "Do you hear me? Nothing!"

Demolisher's voice rang out through the smoky warehouse, shaking walls that were already crumbling and unstable. Venus couldn't help but look toward the wide doorway where she knew Celestial was in a stiff battle against the uranium-enhanced man she knew as Demolisher. Even with the shrill sound permeating the air, she could hear the mammoth man's shout of anger and what sounded like personal pain. She turned back to her own fight, eluding a blast of icy shards emanating from Polar's palm as she catapulted to the other side of the large room.

"You're quick," he said as the shards crashed into the wall. The blocks spurted concrete as the ice drove through them, weakening the already unstable wall. The ceiling above shook, sending down more dust and chunks of debris. He watched her get to her feet and turn on him, her hair wild about her face. "Impressive, for a dead woman."

A victorious smile crossed her face. "You haven't seen anything yet, snowman."

"Is that so?"

She smiled. "You think you can use the elements against me? We on Raydorian Prime mine the stuff." She waved a scarlet arm at the world in general. "On my planet we mine, deep into the planet, and use combat as a form of entertainment." She laughed as he frowned. "And you entertain me!"

He raised his hand and shot a barrage of super-frozen water at her head. She put both hands up, fending off the icy wrath with a blast of Raydorian energy. The two elements met between them in the middle of the room. For a moment, the clash of white ice and brilliant amber energy were at an impasse, neither budging as steam sizzled where they made contact.

Polar laughed as the ice and energy blistered against each other until dropping into orange-tinted water on the cement floor. "Parlor tricks, woman. I've bested bigger minds and stronger men than you. You'll be nothing when I'm through!"

She circled the room as he advanced to one side. She kept the distance between them, trying to find a weakness in his frigid strength. "And achieve what? Your planet's destruction at the hands of these Toroks? This is your world, your kind, and you side with invaders? To what end is that? What do you gain by destroying your homeland?"

He twisted a grin. "Vengeance. That's what I get."

She shook her head, waves of black hair cascading down her shoulders as she stepped to one side, maintaining her distance from him. "Vengeance for what? Who do you blame for your power? The whole of mankind?"

His hands balled into fists, his breath crystallizing in the air as he brought the room's temperature down ten degrees. "Why not?" The careful guardedness he kept in his tone dropped, allowing something less coldhearted to come through. "I didn't ask for this *power* as you call it. Professor Donald's neglect made me this!" He flexed his fingers tighter into fists, raising both arms to his sides like a frozen cross. The air dropped another ten degrees. "I did my job as his assistant in his research -- whatever research he was doing at any time -- and I did a good job at it. I gave up my family, my friends, and my interests to be his assistant. I worked endless hours, under grueling conditions, in Godforsaken places all over this planet. And this?" Every muscle in his body tensed, lowering the room's temperature another ten degrees. "This is what I get? I'm already dead to the world!"

She shook her head, feeling the coldness seep into her as she generated a bit of energy within her body to combat the chill he released. The sound was wearing on her, the high-pitched squeal trapped in her head. It slowly gnawed at her energy reserves as much as the cold emanating from this being capable of controlling the very temperature of the air. "You could have turned this around, couldn't you? If you could become this," she said, gesturing to him with her hand, "couldn't you have put your new power to better use?"

"As what? A circus freak? Some sideshow entertainer?"

"Surely there were other options," she said, seeing an opening to perhaps reason with this very powerful man. "You were once human, as every other human. What was your name? "Then? My name then was Stanley Bennett," he said, his voice losing some of its venom.

Venus smiled more softly. "Have you any family, Stanley Bennett?"

His lips moved, not uttering the words aloud, but she saw them form what she could only guess were names.

"I have no one," he said louder, eyes narrowing on her.

"It looked like you said names." Her head tilted to the side, trying to see more in him than the cold man he'd become. "Was that her earth name Clara? Did you say Clara? Who was she to you? And the other name, Malc--"

"It is better for them to believe Stanley Bennett died in the harsh cold that day in Norway," he said, the tenseness in his body returning like ice running through his veins. "What can you know of cold, woman?"

"I know the mines are cold, and dark," she added. "But you are still alive, Stanley Bennett. You have the power to change things for yourself. You could--"

"I died to the world that day, alone!" He bellowed. He laughed bitterly. "This *power* is a curse!"

He shot a massive wave of ice at her, nearly the size of her entire body. She crouched and held up both hands, fending off the brunt of the glacial attack, but could only slow it down. She felt it push against her wall of Raydorian energy, felt not only the strength of the power but Polar's determination, too. It was a frightening force, his desire to freeze the world the way he'd been frozen out of it. She summoned her inner strength to block his constant attack.

"The world can die, as far as I'm concerned," he said, holding the ice against her, walking slowly to her as she dropped to one knee to block him. "Let it die!"

Her arms shook as she tried to hold back the sheet of cold pressing on her weakening charge of energy. She was fighting not only his abilities, she knew. She was fighting his broken past that no longer held family, and his doomed future.

Onyx knew what a doomed future would look like. She had planned to spend her life with David. She was going to be Mrs. David Ramirez. That was no longer possible, and the Torok across from her in the warehouse's defunct sorting room was the reason. She'd chased after him when he fled and caught up with him here.

Around them, empty tables and a few racks were stationed, but that was all there was to see. The smoke didn't reach this far into the warehouse, but the squealing sound did. Onyx gritted her teeth against it, trying to shut it out.

Zevyn turned on her, seeing he was trapped in the room with no second outlet. He whirled to face her, his pulse cannon in one hand at his side. He laughed as she grimaced in pain from the noise from the reactor plant.

"Can't take a little noise?" He tapped his temple with a gloved hand. "You're with your betters, small human. Run away now before you get hurt."

She shook her head, watching him lower the pulse cannon to cross in front of him. "This will be the last planet you harm, Torok. You'll never succeed."

"Who's going to stop us? You?" He laughed and snapped the cannon up to level at his hip and fired.

She leaped onto a table and flipped off of it to land on the floor behind him. She sent a wide kick to the small of his back, hoping Toroks were anatomically built like humans, and followed with a chop to the side of his head. Then followed with vicious punches to his head. He managed to spin and blocked her hand and caught it, twisting her wrist until she had to back flip to keep her arm from being wrenched from her shoulder socket. The movement broke his grip and she jumped and drove her foot into his neck, then angled up so his head popped back.

He stumbled backward and quickly recovered. He cuffed her under her chin, nearly making her bit her tongue. "You are going to die with this planet!"

Her head snapped back, but she remained on her feet. She spun into him, her back slamming into his chest as she reached over her shoulder and grabbed his grayish yellow jumpsuit at his neck. With all her strength, she curled down and heaved him over her shoulder and sent his body pounding into the concrete floor.

He gasped and jumped to his feet, cocking the cannon up to face her. She kicked its barrel, jerking it from his hands.

"That's your last lucky move," he said, catching his breath as they stared a few feet away from each other. "Now you're going..."

He left off speaking as a loud popping sound came from other rooms in the warehouse.

Onyx could hear the sharp snaps over the shrieking in her head, but it was the expression on the Torok's face that told her that there was a new danger.

Zevyn stepped back and looked around for his cannon. "You're doomed, girl. As well as you can fight, you cannot outrun an explosion. Demolisher placed bombs all over this building. He must be setting them off remotely now."

Onyx's mouth dropped open as she realized what he meant. An explosion ripped through the warehouse, shaking the already unstable walls. Concrete rubble and dust rained down on them.

Zevyn snatched up his weapon from the other side of a table. "You're as good as dead!" He fired off one shot from the cannon at her, but it was weak from a low charge.

She dodged it easily.

"As good as dead!" He ran out of the room.

Another explosion sheared through the air. Onyx crouched and covered her head with her arms as chunks of concrete tumbled from upper floors. Metal pipes banged down and wiring loosened, sending arcs of electricity whipping around. She closed her eyes, and then the whole building shook ferociously.

CHAPTER THIRTEEN

The wads of fabric Tess had stuck in her ears didn't help the shrieking noise much, but did dilute the sound enough for her to think more clearly. She ran through the reactor plant, searching every hallway and open door as she raced on, trying to find the source of power for the enormous core.

She flung open a door to her right, hoping it would lead to a staircase to the core on a lower level or at least a grid room. It was only a closet.

"No," she moaned, her eyes flitting over the assorted brooms and mops, buckets and cleaning supplies on a cart in the dark room. A swift search of the items and shelves gave her no help. She was about to leave when something on the wall caught her attention. She stepped closer.

It was a safety map for emergency situations and procedures, showing the building and cooling towers, the parking lot, and the outlying city around it. The building took up most of the map, showing in yellow the safety exits on the building. Fire extinguishers and phones were circled in yellow and were located on every level with 911 instructions in three languages. The plant was outlined in brown, with the yellow exits, and had the towers marked in orange, the water reservoir in blue, the core itself in red, and the command center in green. The words "YOU ARE HERE" showed an arrow pointing to the closet Tess was in.

She followed the corridors on the map that led from the closet to the control room outlined in green. Next to it, the core was a red square. She put a finger on the command center in green. "That's it," she murmured, nodding. She darted out of the closet. "I'm very close."

An alarm rang through the high-pitched sound now, and a mass of people running at her met Tess as she rounded a corner in the hallway. They were all in hazmat suits, waving for her to turn around.

"Get out!" a woman in a technician's coat yelled as the crowd reached Tess. "The coolant's not working! You must leave!"

Tess pulled away as the woman grabbed her arm and tried to drag her with the fleeing employees.

A man shoved her as the mob nearly carried her away with them in the wrong direction. "Quick, girl! Go!"

Another young man wearing safety glasses and one earplug tried to force her to go with them, but she pushed from him.

"This is an emergency!" he cried, grabbing her again as she slipped away. "You must leave! Come on!"

"Go! Leave!" she said.

He reluctantly did, half-carried away with the rushing crowd.

Tess pulled free from the next few people that tried to help her and fought her way through the crowd hastening for the exits. Once they were past, she sprinted for the control room.

The control center commanded the plant's condenser, generator, and turbine, plus the cooling towers, and the relay system that distributed power to the city utilities. She stopped short outside the glass window that enclosed half of the room. Inside, a hexagon of work stations circled the walls. Even without going inside, she could see the flashing lights and warning signals indicating overloads on nearly every panel.

"So many," she said as her eyes took in the array of lights and consoles. Everything looked important. It was impossible to choose which control was crucial in shutting down the core.

She ran inside and stood in the center of the room, turning to see the flashing warning lights all around her. Most were marked, but with abbreviations she could not understand. She felt the heat from the core as it grew to dangerously high temperatures. There was no way to decide which control would cut off the core and noise. With no choice, she raised her pulse cannon and sprayed a blast of energy at the consoles from left to right and then swept back again.

Smoke leapt from the panels and static charges sprouted like Tesla tentacles, lacing with each other, reaching for her. The blue and yellow electricity arced out, webbing across the panels. A loud surge of the core behind the wall roared in response to the surplus of signals.

There was a loud whooshing sound, and Tess was knocked back against the wall by an invisible punch of energy and then pushed her through the glass windows by a gale force. She was lifted from her feet and dropped at the far wall of the hallway. A wave of hot air and steamy mist followed.

She raised her arm to shield her face, but the air was pushed from her lungs by an unseen pressure, forcing her into an unconscious heap on the floor as the core backed down from a total meltdown.

Amara entered the long, smoky hallway as the last of the power plant workers rushed toward her. A few tried to grab her arm, to take her with them, but she shrugged free.

"Get out!" a woman cried, pulling her arm. "It's toxic!"

"Quickly! Go back!" a man called as Amara eluded his grasp. "Don't go in there!"

"Save yourself!" Amara told them, pushing the woman still reaching for her with the thronging crowd. "Hurry!"

The woman ran on as a few of the escaping workers gave Amara strange looks, eyeing her vivid blue attire. They all ran past her in pursuit of clear air. Their faces were red and pink with lack of good air, and some were frothing as their lungs filled with smoky air. Amara pushed past them and ran down the corridor, listening for any sign of Tess. The high-pitched sound was gone.

It meant that Tess had succeeded.

Amara ran on, hoping the success hadn't cost the young Sundarian her life. She was in a dangerous situation, on a planet foreign to her, and had been drained of natural energy by the Toroks; she had already been through much. A surge of heat wafted toward Amara from a hallway that joined from the left and she ran into it. The smoke got thicker, the heat more intense, and the sound of the core winding down as it burned reached her.

"Tess!" she called, nearly choking on the smoke and fumes. "Tess! Answer me, Tess!"

She made her way into the billowing smoke that funneled to the ceiling. She crouched, finding less smoke hovering there at the floor. She quickly hurried on, still keeping her head lower.

At the turn of a corner, a loud buzzing noise hissed as sparking electrical cords waved wildly. Amara shielded her face with raised arms as she rounded the corner of the hallway. Before her, the whole area was rubble, smoke, fire blazing, and the heavy smell of burning circuitry. She stood to get a better view further into the hall. The shattered glass on the floor meant windows, and she could only hope she was close to the control room.

"Tess! Tess! Where are you?" Amara crouched to waist-height and looked around in the thinner smoke. It took her a few moments to realize she *was* looking at the control room. Now it was melted consoles, blown wiring, and burning walls. The shattered glass covering the floor was nearing the melting points in some places. Beyond what was left of the far wall was a gaping hole, like a cliff, and from it came a mechanical clunking of the turbine, still spinning slowly.

A cough came from the other side of a burning console and Amara hurried there. Behind the computer controls lay Tess, barely alive, the cannon still clutched in one hand, her hair singed and dusty. She was damp with steam and was especially pale. She lay unmoving.

"Tess," Amara called as she knelt beside her. "Tess, it's me, Amara."

Tess' eyes slowly opened, their brown depths now red and sore in the smoky room.

Amara smiled and made a quick study of her. She was splattered with glass and had a few scorch marks on her clothing, but appeared unharmed, mostly knocked out. Amara helped her to sit up, keeping her head below the worst layer of smoke.

"It worked, brave Sundarian," she said, pushing the girl's hair from her cinder-smeared face. "You did good, Tess."

Amara carefully and slowly lifted Tess up. Together they made their way out of the damaged plant's charred hallways. Once in the parking lot, they had their first glimpse of hope. Most of the workers were treating each other, some pulling small pieces of torn clothing out of their ears. Some were making temporary slings out of their sleeves, and some were moving others closer to the ambulance that slowly crawled its way through the parking lot of injured people. They may be a weak specie, Amara decided, but they had heart -- something that could not be measured in the amount of weapons stockpiled or intellectual sophistication.

Tess leaned to Amara's shoulder, their arms at each others' waists as they viewed the parking lot. "They survived."

Amara nodded, surprised and encouraged by the human show of strength. "I think maybe this planet and its people are not as weak as the Toroks think."

Tess coughed and nodded. "But we will still help them?"

"Rightly so, Tess."

Amara took a step away, preparing to transform into her ship form. "Let us join Elandrys and the others. The fight is not yet over, Tess."

Onyx chased Zevyn through the trembling warehouse hallways as the building shook. The dust was heavy in the air, making seeing him difficult. He took a metal staircase up to the next level where the deck opened over the trucking bay below. She followed, keeping her bearings as to where she was in the building, not wanting to get trapped and surprised on the grate-floor level.

Suddenly the shrieking noise stopped. The air seemed lighter, and the rumbling in the walls eased.

Onyx slowed, sensing the difference. She looked to where Zevyn had also halted and was now looking at her from across the mostly empty second floor. The catwalk of metal grate floor allowed the dust to sift through to the bay below, making the air clear more quickly.

She smiled, steadily crossing the metal grate floor. "Looks like your little trick is over. Things didn't go as planned, wouldn't you say?"

He charged his pulse cannon, facing her. "All is not lost." He raised the barrel, aiming at her. "And you're good as dead!"

He fired the cannon, but only a low buzz came from it. He shook it and pulled the trigger again. Nothing.

Onyx laughed, shaking her head as he squeezed the trigger repeatedly, his frustration growing. "Empty! You're used up, Torok! Out of juice!"

He sent her a snarling scowl, and then put a hand on the rail running around the loft. He leaped and dropped over the side. He landed near one of the cement bays below and slipped under the half-raised semi-truck door.

Onyx sprung over the side of the rail and landed near where Zevyn had. She warily crouched under the door and looked around at the concrete bay exterior. It was empty.

Both cargo decks were empty. Her eyes went over the cement barrier that ran around the back of the warehouse, but she saw no one. The Torok had simply disappeared.

"You could say that's a win, wouldn't you?" came Celestial's triumphant tone from the warehouse depths. "It looks like victory to me" answer Onyx.

Onyx turned back to look at the bay door. The noise was gone and the only sounds now were conquering cries from those beings Amara had brought back from the Realm of the Immortals. The battles were over, the odds now evened with the shrieking sound extinguished. Onyx smiled. Fate had dealt a level battlefield.

"Or Amara and the girl, Tess, have leveled it for us," Onyx said to herself as she smiled. She could hear Celestial speaking inside, his voice stronger now.

A moment later, police sirens rose from the other side of the building. They were soon joined by Global Security Alliance agents calling out to each other as they surrounded the premises.

Onyx breathed easier, and hurried to the front of the warehouse.

By the time Amara and Tess got back inside the warehouse, the shrill sound from the plant blast had ended.

And, Amara was happy to see, Chaos has lost their battle.

She and Tess hurried into the warehouse main room where half of one wall was blown out. Polar was on his knees and struggling to get up, with Venus standing nearby. Her hands wielded Raydorian surges of energy from each palm. Polar was steaming, his back wet and half frozen, his movements sluggish as the woman before him kept him at bay with non-lethal blasts of energy.

Celestial was also in the room, somewhat dented in spirit, but with Demolisher losing their very physical fight. Without the noise giving Chaos the advantage, the three warriors from the Realm of the Immortals were at full power.

The odds had been evened.

No sooner had Amara and Tess appeared in the room, than Kelvar, still bloodied, joined looking at his comrades. He stood in the doorway as the smoke cleared, searching the scene for Zevyn.

Elandrys was just delivering a near-lethal punch to Mystic, who was limp from casting spells. He folded and backed to the wall, shaking his head as blood gushed from his nose.

Tess raised her cannon and fired, hitting Demolisher, taking the fullest brunt of force he fell backwards limp to the floor. She sent a second blast at Wraith Blade and Mystic, but Wraith Blade leapt out of range. Mystic wasn't quite so lucky, but he did escape most of the damage as he dove over the side of the blasted wall.

Amara raced to Elandrys' side as he watched Mystic disappear over the wall. He turned to her. "You sent great power from the Realm of the Immortals. We certainly needed their help."

She placed her hand on his arm, her eyes searching his face that was starting to bruise near one eye. "You've fought a good fight, Elandrys." She looked to where Tess was lowering her weapon and nudging Demolisher's slumped body. "Both Sundarians did well."

A loud whine of sirens cut the air and tires screeching to a stop outside made them all look to the door in one still intact wall.

"Come out with your hands up!" a militaristic voice demanded from outside. "Throw your weapons on the ground and come out with your hands up!"

"Policemen," Tess said, curious and alarmed. She looked to one window as footsteps were heard there. "A police squad. I've heard the Toroks talk about them, laugh about them. There is a large vehicle with men in black attire running around."

"We have to get out of here. It's going to be difficult to explain to the police exactly who you are. There is going to be a lot of questioning and they are going to want to take all of you into custody."

Elandrys glanced to Polar, who was lying on the floor, moaning in near unconsciousness. "Do you think they can handle them now?" asked Elandrys.

"They are going to have to."

"Let's go!"

Gimel Stone, Celestial, and Venus were the first to leap into the hole scorched in the three-story ceiling. Elandrys, Amara, and Tess followed. Onyx looking around, was the last to exit.

Once on the rooftop, they knelt and looked over the edge of the building.

Below, three squad cars and now a S.W.A.T. MRAP were arranged in an arc in the parking lot as officers and men in black gear stealthily made their way around the warehouse. A man with a bullhorn in one hand and radio in his other hand was looking at the hole in the wall, awaiting trouble.

"Look," Tess said, pointing.

They all watched as four Global Security Alliance agents ushered Polar and Demolisher, both heavily confined in handcuffs, from the building to the waiting armored vehicle. Demolisher had two heavy-duty tazer points sticking out of his back.

Celestial looked to Venus and Elandrys, and then turned to Gimel Stone. "I did not see the Toroks among the detained men."

Elandrys and Amara exchanged uneasy looks, their thoughts aligned. "Nor Wraith Blade or Mystic," she said.

The sounds of something scrambling over the opposite side of the warehouse rooftop made them all turn to look there, ready for the Toroks to appear.

Elandrys and Amara backed away from the roof edge.

"You did a good job today," he said, offering a smile to Onyx."

Amara nodded to Onyx, smiling. "We must get away and see to our injuries."

She raised her arms to the sky. Amara transformed and everyone boarded her. Once inside, Amara lifted into the smoky sky.

Amara hovered over Lincoln City below, staying out of sight as the authorities finished up their business at the warehouse.

An ambulance slowly circled the parking lot before leaving. The Global Security Alliance vehicle had already taken its burden of Demolisher and Polar away, leaving half of the S.W.A.T team members in black riot gear to aide the police officers searching the building.

Amara distributed her ready supply of first aid needs to Venus, who was helping Onyx bandage her left arm and calf muscle. Celestial was mostly weary, depleted in energy and keeping his armor intact, and so sat slumped in one of the larger chairs at the viewing window. Tess' injuries were mostly superficial, plus a stellar headache from the blast of taking out the plant reactor. She also had small cuts and pinpoints of burn marks from the backlash. The small tape of ointment Venus touched to Tess' skin seemed to work miraculously, removing the small burns on the spot and closing the tiny cuts.

Tess smiled as her wounds nearly disappeared. "That's remarkable."

Amara finished tying a bandage around Elandrys' large bicep. "I've picked up the best supplies from all parts of the galaxy. I know you've already fought side by side for the same cause, but, Elandrys, this is Venus from the planet Raydoria," she said, nodding to the woman tending Tess. "And Gimel, from the planet Za'Bal, and Celestial from the Immortal galaxy." She indicated the last man, who gave Elandrys a salute. Amara sighed. "The Immortals sent them to help us."

Elandrys looked to each of them. "It is greatly appreciated. I am honored to know you all."

Amara looked to Tess, who was running her hand over her now smooth skin after Venus' treatment. "This is Tess, a Sundarian also."

"You took out the reactor," Gimel Stone said with a broad smile. "Nicely done."

Tess blushed a bit, but smiled at him.

Celestial leaned to look out the viewing window, his eyes on the scene below. "I don't see any of the Toroks captured."

Elandrys met him there and looked out. "I think the Toroks got away."

They watched the warehouse below, seeing officers still milling about, bringing out evidence. Now a fire truck was entering the lot gates.

Venus joined them, as did the rest, all looking out the port window. "The threat is still here," she said. "We failed."

"We prevented them from destroying Earth for now, and saved Tess," Elandrys said, glancing to the girl. He looked around at them all. "I could not have asked for better warriors."

Onyx followed his gaze, her attention resting on each individually. "What you have done... I don't even know how to begin to thank all of you."

Onyx takes off her mask. Her faces is badly soiled and her hair is frizzled and dusty. Onyx sits back in the chair and close her eyes.

"Earth is on the path of the Toroks. I will try to establish forms of interstellar communication with this planet. If you should ever need me again, I will be here for you," Gimel Stone said sincerely.

"Thank you. But why?""

"Because we have been given a chance to help someone else," Elandrys answered. "We were helped to win our war. That's how life should be. As Gimel said, we will be here again should you need us."

Venus gripped Onyx's arm above her bandage, squeezing a friendly assurance. "I as well."

Celestial was still looking out the window, his eyes taking in the trees and sunshine spreading long shadows over the warehouse. "Me, too. This planet is a fascination to me. Have faith, my friend." He sent Onyx a quick glance. "We have begun a course of victory together."

Onyx was in awe of the beings around her. Not only were they superhuman in strength and abilities, but they also had compassion and intelligence to match. What she had seen with this dove blue clad woman was amazing.

Transforming from a flesh and blood being into a spaceship? Impossible. She never would have believed it had she not seen it firsthand.

"Amara," she said, "you are incredible. Of course you're not human, but what...?"

"My creator is unknown," Amara said kindly, reading the expression on Onyx's face. "I explore and record all that I have seen, which seems to be my purpose. I have vast knowledge of space and the life therein."

Onyx was still astonished. She shook her head slowly, gazing out the viewing window, and murmured, "Who would have thought I would ever meet anyone from another world who would help me save my world?"

"You must alert the authorities of your planet about the presence and threat of the Toroks. They are brutal as you well know, and they mean only to enslave or destroy" said Elandrys to Onyx. "Use every available resource you have to find them, and capture them."

Amara looked to Elandrys standing beside her, feeling his arm encircle her waist. "I know the Immortals have given you all transportation pods," she said to the warriors that had joined her from the Realm of the Immortals, "but it would be my great pleasure to take you to your home planets myself."

Elandrys' arm tightened on her waist as he addressed the out-worlders. "It would give Amara many myself a chance to get to know you."

Amara looked up at the clouds above them. "And for me to see more of the phenomenon of space."

CHAPTER FOURTEEN

Wraith Blade has been here before. She knows how to escape. Wraith Blade has made it to the outside of the building. She has climb along the side of the building and lowered herself to the ground using the old rusty fire escape.

Where is everyone? The last explosion cause everyone to run out of the collapsing building.

Red and yellow-orange flames are coming out of the windows and dark smoke is filling the area.

Wraith Blade has made it to the bottom of the building looking for her friends. The Toroks are no where to be seen.

Policemen, firemen, and a S.W.A.T. team are converging on the building.

There she sees him, the man she still loves. Global Security Alliance agent Devante Marcelle. He is a member of the Global Security Alliance that are now also arriving. He is with other Global Security Alliance agents. Wraith Blade is frozen in her tracks.

She both loves him and hates him. Those crossed feelings instantly consumes her while she stands there looking at him, while he is unaware of her presence. This is the man she used to love with all her heart. This is the man that broke her heart. Wrath Blade just looks at him as he moves into the building with more agents.

Movement behind her causes her to turn at once. He made it out also. Mystic, is he is the only one left from the team?

Wraith Blade runs to him. He is bloodied and stumbling, he can barely walk. He is badly injured.

Mystic will be able to heal himself once he regains his strength. Now he is helpless, Wraith Blade has scarcely a scratch on her. They need to escape without delay.

Wraith Blade puts Mystic arm over her shoulder and takes his weight.

"Come on, we have to move." Wraith Blade says to him. However Mystic eyes sees his friends.

"Look there is Demolisher and Polar, we have to save them" Mystic says struggling to move towards them.

Wrath pulls him back. "No! Think, there is too many of them the police, S.W.A.T teams and GSA. You are weak and injured. We have to leave, we have to escape."

"But we can't just leave them. They are our friends."

"And risk being captured ourselves. More police are coming to investigate. More GSA agents will be coming too. I know it. We can save them later. We know where they are being taken. We can save them when we find the Toroks."

Wraith Blade moves Mystic along the shadowy alleyway, hoping to avoid detection.

that everything total failed for Mystic and myself? Wraith Blade thinks to herself as she is watching both the back and front for the appearance of ant stray police.

"What happens to us now" asked Wraith Blade. "Everything failed. Everything!"

"We regroup and plan. I don't see the Toroks so that means they probably weren't captured. We'll find them too. There is still a chance for us."

Mystic leans on Wraith Blade behind the alley in the corner. They watch as Demolisher and Polar are loaded into an armored van.

"He is here isn't he? The cop guy you're in love with. He's here?" Wraith Blade tried to move Mystic along down the alley. She doesn't answer. "You can't face him can you? You cant even look at him too long?"

Wraith Blade is still silent. Wraith Blade helps Mystic into a crowd of people. There is turmoil on the streets. People are injured and laying on the ground.

Wraith Blade keeps looking around to see if anyone notices them.

Wraith Blade soon sees a coat on the ground. She takes it and Mystic puts it on. It is staring to rain. There are also abandon umbrellas laying next to some of the people on the ground waiting for medical attention.

Wraith Blade takes one and holds it over their heads. "Just a little further down this street. We should be in the clear" says Wraith Blade.

Mystic moves with Wraith Blade. They watch as more police cars come and ambulances appear on the area. Wraith Blade and Mystic get to the corner, cautiously looks down the block, it's clear. They walk a few feet into the block.

There are many cars on the streets. Many good Samaritans. Many careless people also.

"Look." Wraith Blade points to a car with the keys still inside. Mystic instantly knew what she was thinking.

Mystic musters up his strength as Wraith Blade helps him into the driver's seat.

Wraith Blade runs quickly to the other side still looking around for people who may notice them. Mystic drives down the street. It's getting dark and it's starting to drizzle more heavily. It doesn't matter to Mystic or Wrath Blade, they escape.

Kelvar could barely keep up with Zevyn as they lumbered toward the trees at the back of the warehouse lot. A cement culvert, broken and two feet deep, opened before them, covered in weeds and muddy brown water runoff from the sewers.

"Slow down," he grunted as Zevyn outpaced him. He grabbed a small tree trunk as he nearly fell into the culvert, his knees ready to collapse.

"Hurry up!" Zevyn called back, easily leaping the cement ditch. He glanced back at the tree that hid the warehouse.

The squealing sound had ended, but now police sirens took up the airwaves. Screeching tires and shouts from the S.W.A.T. team could still be heard.

Zevyn turned and ran.

Kelvar carefully maneuvered the culvert and climbed up the slope on the other side. Here the trees were thicker and helped hide them and give him handholds as he wobbled.

"You let yourself get nearly killed," Zevyn grunted as Kelvar caught up with him.

They picked their way through the tall weeds and spiny shrubs that dissolved into tall, thicker trees at the city's edge.

"Yeah, well, that Sundarian guy knew what he was doing." Kelvar wiped a hand over his face. It was no longer numb; the swelling had begun on the left side of his face and his nose was broken. Bruising spread from his left cheek to his right eye and dried blood matted his eyebrows and caked his lips. He spat out a froth of blood as they passed a short evergreen tree. "We'd have won if they didn't get reinforcements."

Zevyn nodded, making their way through the dense trees. "We're close."

From the trees, a tunnel six feet high emerged. It was an overflow drainage tunnel, seldom used now that the river was rerouted to the other side of the city for hydropower. It was a handy route back to where their spacecraft waited. It was operational, ready to get off this planet, but they still had a few loose ends to tie up.

The coolness of the tunnel would hide them from any police helicopter searching the power plant and warehouse area, but so far, they hadn't heard any.

"With the chaos in the city, any emergency crafts will be used for humans." Zevyn coughed as his lungs filled with fluid.

"Yeah, Chaos," Kelvar grunted as they cleared the tunnel. "They were handy."

He pushed back the thick curtain of pine boughs that drooped over their path to expose a clearing in the woods.

Before them squatted their Torok air cruiser, now repaired enough to lift off, and so far, undiscovered by the city dwellers. It was a first class cruiser in the Torok space lines, and they had never been happier to see it.

Zevyn checked the landing gear and cannons on either side, and then ran a hand over the gunmetal gray finish. "Were the worms downloaded into the military arms computer system complete?"

Kelvar nodded as he opened the fighter's hatch. "Yes. The transmission was sent."

They climbed into the hatch and shut it, locked it, and made their way to the cockpit. Kelvar stripped off his bloody armor and gloves, grimacing as the movement opened several cuts on his jaw.

Zevyn dropped into the cockpit crew chair and flipped several switches. On one screen, the fuel sources powered up.

Kelvar leaned over and extended his hand. Zevyn glanced at his palm.

"Look at these little babies," Kelvar said.

Zevyn looked at the small diamonds. He scowled. "What? Souvenirs from this place?"

"No, not souvenirs." Kelvar let the diamonds roll on his palm. "Polar gave me these in that jewelry heist we did. I accidentally left them in the weapons module and discovered they powered our weapons flawlessly." He grinned at Zevyn's surprise. "I now have our power source we were looking for on this planet."

Zevyn gave the small stones a longer study. "They're carbon-based?"

"Yes. Finally, we have an energy source that is stable and unlimited for us to use." Kelvar pointed to the screen where the engines were showing full power. "They will work our weapons and systems perfectly."

Zevyn sat back in his seat, watching the computers and systems come online. "Oh, what great plans we have for this planet. I just cannot wait."

"Yeah, Demolisher did a superb job of hiding our presence and the computer worms at the central arms computers." Kelvar placed the diamonds in a small tube on the console and capped it. "All we have to do now is remotely trigger the computer warhead worms remotely."

"What about Demolisher and Polar?" Zevyn nodded to the view window in front of the cockpit. It showed only woods and brush, but a mile beyond was the warehouse. "They got taken by the human authorities. What do we do about them?"

Kelvar wasn't concerned. "Minor setbacks. The warhead made contact with the nuclear rector plant. The message was sent to our home planet." He found a tube of wound treatment in the first aid kit under the console. "They now know of our location and information about Earth. An attack will be prepared and launched. We can soon hold the planet captive, once we find a place to setup."

Zevyn nodded, grinning at the idea. "I like it."

"Until then," Kelvar said as Zevyn readied the craft to lift off, "we find a better place to lay low."

Zevyn enacted the craft's low atmosphere cloaking shields. "And await orders from Toria."

By the time *Amara* took everyone back to Maria's apartment and Onyx was again feeling more like *Maria* than her alter ego, it was late afternoon and growing cloudy outside.

And, Maria realized, days had passed.

The apartment seemed so small with all her newfound friends crowding the living room and kitchen. They were all tall, broad, stoutly built, and strong. She felt small beside them, but, as she'd proven over their last battles together, she wasn't weak.

She wasn't quite their caliber -- yet -- but she was learning.

Celestial ducked his head beneath the ceiling fan, looking around with wonder at her books and pictures. "Is this how all human women live?"

Maria nodded. "Mostly. Everyone's place varies, according to personal taste, but yes, I'm normal."

Elandrys looked to where Maria's cell phone lay beside her answering machine. A light was blinking, indicating several messages. "I think you have a malfunction."

"Oh, that," Maria said, skirting Venus and Gimel Stone, who were also looking at the device. "It's probably the...my dad, or...hospital."

So much had happened.

She pushed the message button. "I know you're still upset, baby, but call me. Your mother is doing better and can see visitors. She needs to see you."

Maria fought back tears, tears of both anguish and joy at her father's words.

There was a beep and then Camille's voice came over the machine. "Where are you, girl? You got us worried sick. No one has seen you since, you know...that night. You didn't even show for David's burial. I know all that has happened is probably hard on you. Wherever you are, call somebody. Please!"

Amara stepped closer to her. "Your mother is going to recover?"

Maria exhaled a trembling sigh. "I think so." She wiped her eyes, refusing to cry among these tough other-worlders. She looked to Celestial, who was staring at a newspaper on the kitchen table. He seemed to be trying to read it, but couldn't decipher the foreign characters.

She went to the table and picked up the paper. Obviously, Camille had been by. The page was open to the obituaries. David's face looked back at her, his photo from a recent party. She wasn't in it. It felt surreal to her.

Celestial was watching her closely. "Do you know him?"

She nodded, feeling a rush of emotions flood her. She felt Tess' hand on her shoulder as she looked back to Amara. "Can I ask one favor of you, Amara?"

By the time they got to the cemetery where David had been buried many days before, it was nearly dark and raining. The sky was deep gray, with only a few stars looking down on the collection of mourners making their way to the recent gravesite. Maria had her long, charcoal gray trench coat pulled around her slender form, still wearing her Onyx attire, as she walked with Elandrys, Amara, Tess, Venus, Celestial, and Gimel Stone. As they had carefully passed the first few grave markers, Celestial had been full of questions -- why some were so large, so ornate, so heavy, so hideous, so small, so plain -- until Venus gently told him she would try to explain at another time. Now was a time of reverence.

Maria was barely aware of the talk among them, conscious only of the modest gravestone at the mound of dirt marking David's resting place. She stopped at it, as the others stood a few feet back, cluing in on propriety for the moment.

She knelt down, silently reading the short inscription on the stone. "He was a good man, a really good man, trying to do what is right." She sighed, fighting guilt and despair. "I was not even here for the burial." She kneeled on the wet ground. She touched the headstone, the stopping point to what was supposed to be their life together. "I loved him. I'm going to miss him so much, more than he will ever know."

Elandrys stepped forward and knelled beside her. "I wish we could have done more to help you find David's killers. I am so sorry. I wish we could even stay, but Tess family may have the horrible realization that their daughter is dead. I must return her back home to her family. I wish I could have done more. I really do wish could stay. Even to help comfort you through this time of mourning."

She felt a comfort as his presence, his words. "You have done more than enough. You saved Earth from an invasion and rescued a pretty amazing little girl."

Tess smiled a little when Maria looked to her. "You won't ever forget us, will you?"

Maria stood and returned a soft smile. And Elandrys stood with here. "Of course not."

Tess took off the Sundarian necklace from around her neck and placed it in Maria's palm. "For you."

Maria turned the metal chain in her hand. The pendant was a coil of circles around a hematite round, fastened to the chain. The metal of the pendant and chain was gunmetal in color, but changed to silvery steel, copper-gold, and then brassy bronze as she turned it. It was unlike any metal she'd ever seen. "It is so beautiful. Thank you."

Tess smiled wide.

Maria hugged her. "With all that has happened," she said, addressing them all, "I just realized I'm talking to people from other planets, another galaxy, and other races."

Elandrys nodded. "Me, too. You are a remarkable woman. A gallant warrior. It was an honor to meet you. Believe that justice will have its place and time for David. I wish I could tell you what to do, but I cannot. You will have to choose which road you take now. This I do know: hatred and revenge will eat you up inside. You are wise and strong, and I know you will make the right decisions." He smiled. "My first Earth friend and we don't know your name."

Maria felt suddenly more human than ever, and at the same time, stronger for the Sundarian's recognition of her strengths. It is starting to lightly rain again. Maria now feeling the damp air fully on her face. Her face and hair so dreadfully soiled. "My name is Maria, Maria Velasquez. Soon the world will know me as Onyx." Venus, Celestial, and Gimel Stone nodded, smiling a little. Maria smiled back, and then turned to Elandrys and Amara. "So, you think I will ever see you again?"

"Maybe, my friend," he said.

"Maria," Amara said, seeming to like the sound of the name, "we were there to help each other. Somehow, even in the immensity of space, I know we will meet again."

Maria embraced her, feeling as if she had reunited with a long lost friend, and then moved to Elandrys, and then Tess again. It took a few moments to hug everyone goodbye, with well-wishes and murmurs of friendship from all, even Gimel Stone, and then, they had to leave.

Amara transformed into her spaceship form and Elandrys, Tess, Venus, Celestial, and Gimel Stone boarded and the craft rose into the rainy sky. Maria watched them ascend, feeling the soft rain gentle on her face as she watched *Amara* fade smaller in the dark heavens until it was only a pinpoint of light like any other star.

And then, she was gone.

The rain was the only sound now, splattering on gravestones and splashing on the few trees. Maria looked back to David's grave. She felt more alone than ever. Despite the Sundarian's words, she could feel the sense of vengeance creep into her soul. It was a bitter feeling -- young bitterness not wholly ripened -- a seedling that she knew would grow.

Maria kneeled back on the ground, beside David's tombstone. She lets what has happened in the past few days flood her mind.

Maria closes her eyes. David's face flashes in front of her. Images of their last moments together, his last kiss becomes a treasured memory for her.

Maria let the soft rain blend in with the tears that were now flowing out of her eyes.

Nevertheless, against Elandrys warning, hatred saturates her soul. "I promise you, I will not rest until I avenge you, David," she said quietly. "To those who are responsible for your death, be warned," she said louder, more pointedly as she looked up into the dark night. "For I am Onyx, and I'm coming for you."

Now deep in space, and maybe almost a million light years away from earth, Elandrys sits in stillness. He is staring as the bright stars and colorful suns pass in the dark front port window.

Elandrys came into space to find solitude in the vast darkness of space. Be he did not. The threat of the Toroks is still present.

What will become of earth, what will become of his new friend Maria?

Elandrys and everyone knows, earth is now a target for the Toroks conquest and even destruction. The Toroks were not captured. What could he possible do to save earth?

Sundaria has just recovered from the bloody battle with the Toroks. They are unprepared even to make the voyage to earth. Should the Toroks attack now, earth will fall to the assault of the Toroks.

Amara glimpses over to Elandrys, she takes his hand. She knows him well, she knows what he is feeling right now. He will not accept this victory. Elandrys is plagued by the crosswords of decisions. However, she is willing to face the uncertainly that lies ahead. She also knows she will never leave his side.

Gimel, Celestial, and Venus rest their bodies as well as their minds for the long journey home.

Tess has been through a ordeal that she would soon want to forget. Be she has survived. She is a Sundarian.

Could Elandrys ask them to risk their lives again? This was not a full Torok attack, from what he knows about the Toroks, the next time it will be.

THE END

ELANDRYS, THE SUNDARIAN

The Sundarians were created by a cosmic life form energy called the Nebula. The Nebula encircles Sundaria like a ring in the planet's atmosphere. The planet is hidden away deep within the mysterious Sulaiman galaxy.

Elandrys was born the son of Ajani and Credenda on Sundaria.

Elandrys father Ajani was serving in the Sundarian military when he was born.

Elandrys mother Credena has studied Medical technology and was a nurse and primary teacher in the Northern Providence.

Elandrys was raised with his family in a large house in a small, peaceful farming village. His family, older brother Denarius, cousin Okemah, uncle Kali, and Aunt McKenna, and members of the village were all close-knit. They shared many days together dancing and singing, and sports competitions were often held once their day's work was finished.

Elandrys older brother Denarius, was fond of hunting and weapons at a early age he finished school and joined the Sundarian Military like his father.

The family loved to hear their cousin Okemah singing in the late evening time. Okemah had a voice of an angel.

Okemah traveled all over Sundaria singing in the villages. She had become the requested singer for many special events.

Elandrys studied Agricultural Sciences and graduated, like most of the boys in his village. He became a simple agricultural farmer like most of his family and the people that lived in his small village. He also spent time learning hand-to-hand combat and bodybuilding from the military after his work day was finished. His older brother, Denarius, had thought it would be good for Elandrys to know how to defend himself, too. This gave the brothers time to spend together as well.

Elandrys learned many wise lessons from his mother and father. It helped build Elandrys' character and gave him a moral focus. He grew into a respectable, reserved man, and later developed into a mighty warrior.

Elandrys traveled only once on the cultural space expedition which is customary for all Sundarians. There he saw the nearby loosely populated planet. That is where he developed his desire to venture into space.

Elandrys seldom traveled outside of his village, usually only on special occasions or when horseback riding with his brother and cousins. At a young age, curiosity gave him a desire to travel outside of the Sundaria atmosphere and into space to learn of some of the mysteries of space. This desire persisted as he got older and became a man.

The Toroks invaded Sundaria seeking to harness the power of the Nebula stars that encircled Sundaria.

Elandrys helped in the military and lead small troops of Sundarian defense forces against the Toroks in what became an all out battle.

Elandrys was the first Sundarian to have contact with the Nebula encircling the planet. He learned that the Nebula was also a life form and was intelligent. The Nebula led Elandrys in defeating the Torok invaders.

Once the Sundarians learned more about the Nebula, they discovered that each Sundarian had the power of the Nebula energy inside them and that they could control this manifestation. This also helped in defeating the Toroks during the war.

Elandrys learned to shoot energy from his hands. The Sundarians also learned how to power their technology with the energy of the Nebula. They skillfully used this to enhance their weapons so that only they could control the Nebula stars' energy.

The Sundarians, through study and research, also learned that joining two Nebula stars together formed a new energy source. This knowledge help them create technology that only they could operate should they be invaded again.

The Sundarians lived in peace with the Nebula as their technology progressed.

Now a sphere of Nebula energy force field surrounds and protects the people of Sundaria.

During the war, Elandrys met Amara -- a being who was both a woman and a living space explorer ship.

Elandrys fell in love with Amara and asked her to join him in his space exploration.

Amara loved Elandrys as well and accepted his request. Elandrys left Sundaria with Amara and they ventured into space, learning countless things and seeing the imaginable.

AMARA

Shape shifting, or metamorphosis is the ability of an entity to physically transform into another being or form. This is usually achieved through an inherent faculty of a mythological creature, divine intervention, or the use of magic spells or talismans. This is not who Amara is.

Amara is a living space explorer ship. Her creator and origin are unknown.

Amara came to consciousness in outer space in the Mali Solar System. Amara has search her data-bases recording and found she is a created being of cosmic energy.

Amara is both ship and woman. She can also project real, life-like illusions of herself.

As a ship, Amara can create and shift seats and tables for the number of passengers she may have.

Amara has a small medical station to help all injured life forms she may encounter.

Amara also has probes which she can send to scan and record in places where can not be. Amara can get instantaneous visuals, sounds, and recordings from these probes.

Amara has no weapons, but has advance stealth capacities to hide herself in times of detrimental predicaments.

She can be injured as a woman and damaged as a ship. She has an internal self-preservation system that allows her to be repaired if any part of her becomes damaged while in human or in ship form.

Her internal functions are that of a ship's inner mechanism with an organic computer processor system.

Amara has total control of all her ships systems and functions. Amara can function as a human woman but does not have reproduction capabilities.

In woman form, Amara's body skin is made up of a unique organic material. She does as a cosmic amber color energy that flows through her body. She can exist in all forms of atmospheres. She is in control of all her human systems as well. She does not age; she lives off renewable cosmic power cells.

Amara's outer clothing is a thin powered cloak exoskeleton. The colors of her clothing and her outer shell as a ship are alike. They are made of unknown, resilient materials bolstered by a cosmic energy source. She can remove her powered exoskeleton clothes and put on other clothing when she is in full woman form.

Amara does display a women's maternal instincts, cultivating manners, and virtuousness.

Amara is highly intelligent and is said to be a profound teacher because of the vast knowledge that she has.

Amara is attractive looking by any cultures standard of beauty.

Amara stands about five feet and four inches high. She has round hazel colored eyes that can change shape to allow her to see in any atmosphere, water, and darkness.

Amara has a semi-muscular build, with long black hair down to her shoulders.

Amara's compassionate nature and exploration computer systems encoding directs her to document every planet, solar system, organic life form, galaxy, and universe in existence -- virtually everything she comes in contact with -- creating a vast information database. She has advanced sensors, immense intelligence, languages ability, scanning abilities, and force fields, and can travel more rapidly that the unbelievable speed of light.

Amara does have to heat and drink. In human form of more then twenty-four of earth like hours, if she not eaten anything edible and organic, her body will shut-down, and her energy cells will recharge her.

Amara has traveled for many eons in space. She has seen universes, galaxies, and solar systems. She has seen birth of various life forms and death of many also. She has cultivated civilizations.

Amara has encountered many persons of indescribable existence and origins.

She has recorded a vast amount of data from the entire universe.

Amara has learned millions of languages, cultures, advance medical, and science technologies.

There is still many mysteries that the vast space hold that she has not seen and recorded.

Over time, after seeing so many cultures, so many wonders, Amara did not know where she fit in. There was no one like her.

Amara searched the dark vast endless space for someone that was even similar to her. With all the beings she had met, with all the things she has experienced, over the many years, she grew highly despondent and intensely lonely. Amara found no one that she could unite with.

Amara is a unique creation with no clear reason and purpose for her existence.

While traveling through space, she happened to see the Sundarians waging war against the attack of the Toroks. She was impressed with the valor of the Sundarians and Elandrys, and stayed to help fight in the war.

For Amara, Elandrys stood out. Even though he is humanoid by her standards, there were something about him that touched her *heart and soul.*

After the war Amara and Elandrys become friends during that time.

After the war was over, with the Sundarians the victors, a massive planetary reconstruction took place, and peace again reigned on Sundaria.

Amara stayed on Sundaria to help with the reconstruction and became a medical aid for the Sundarians.

However, the brutal war and massive death left a longing to escape all the pain and suffering Elandrys had seen.

Elandrys expressed to Amara his craving to travel in the stars. She chose to join his expedition through space as his companion.

THE TOROKS, FROM PLANET TORIA

The planet Toria is located in a desolate solar system. It is overwhelmingly covered with an excessive amount of defensive mines, communication satellites, and ready space fighters moving in the atmosphere.

Toria is 15.8 times bigger than Earth and its gravity is about 5.36 times that of Earth.

A single day lasts 42.67 hours and a year lasts 494 days.

The planet is made up of 5 connecting planets. No moons are suns orbit the planet Toria.

The plant-like organisms on this planet are primarily shrubs and smaller trees, supported by small flowers, grasses and fungi on the bottom layer. Tall trees make up only a small portion of plant life on this planet.

The species on this planet may not be much more than the first steps to specialized species, this doesn't take anything away from their astonishing beauty and elegance.

Just like the surface, the underwater world doesn't have much more to offer than basic plants. While they do play an important role in many of the planet's eco-systems, they're not that spectacular to look at.

There is a vivid three gray, red, and orange sun configuration that circles the planets inner surroundings. The climate on that planet is very warm, with very little rainfall. It has tremendous rock formations all throughout the planet.

The planet has a substantial accumulation of vegetation that is transformed into various complex dry organics and use for food.

It is a highly advance industrial planet. Massive warehouses of machinery, weapons development, and complex automations operations are habitually all over the exterior of the planet. Unmanned robotics are all along the surface of Toria, moving crates, and working systematic assembly lines.

Many of these vast warehouses are covered with armored dome casings.

Underground there are multi species slave compartment cells for species captured as prisoners of war. They work the functions that the machines are unable to.

The male and female population both are at an identical number, however there are no female Toroks on the Toria command center.

The only thing coming close to animals on the planet are the many species of microorganisms found on pretty much every surface of this planet. While they may not provide a spectacular sight for the eyes, they do show promises of higher forms of life being possible on this planet.

Corals, although very basic, can be found all over the planet's oceans, seas and lakes. While they lack the bright colors and odd shapes you'd find on Earth's corals, they do have the makings of a varied aquatic wildlife, with an abundance of gorgeous species.

The aquatic organisms aren't very large in numbers, but they are huge in size. They can grow to sizes of nearly 100 meters and a diameter of up to 5 meters. These underwater giants give this aquatic world an eerie atmosphere as you never know what could lurk behind that pillar. But at the same time, they provide homes to thousands of species on all depths, which makes studying even 1 giant coral an absolute delight.

As expected, the only life forms coming close to being animals are the millions of microorganisms found pretty much everywhere.

Toroks live on the industrialized planet Toria. No man is believed to have ever been on Toria.

When the outpost colony planet reaches a certain amount of Toroks, the surpluses of Toroks are moved to another outpost colony planet. This pattern is followed each time the Toroks conquer a planet.

In the city at the center of Toria is the gray reinforced brightly lit steel highly active Torok central command center. It reaches to a height of twenty-five stories.

The building in it's spherical and inter joining rectangular design has high frequency interstellar massive communication satellites on top of the building and a huge landing bay to the right side of the building.

The central command center is also an essential haven for shuttles moving about Toria.

There are billions of strategic Torok space station outpost colonies throughout the galaxies and solar systems.

The Toroks are known to have only a commanding leadership. Commands are sent from the commanding leadership and relayed to Toroks and Torok outposts.

Not much is known about Toria laws, government, religion, marriage customs, mating, money systems, and their origins.

Toroks are massive in size, all about six feet tall. There skin is dark and they have brown curly hair that usually extends down past their broad shoulders.

Their average lifespan is 150 years and a Torok in good physical condition possesses strength, reaction time, speed, and endurance greater than the finest of human being.

A Torok who is in excellent physical shape can lift one half ton and are physically slightly superior to the peak of normal human physical achievement.

Exactly what the Toroks eat is unknown and they will generally eat any food that will sustain them. The Toroks are physically very strong, and stand about seven feet tall in height. They are trained at early ages for combat, scientific development, torture techniques, and survival skills.

Toroks have no known sickness, hereditary diseases, are physical deformities.

The women are trained to go into battle when necessary, but are not often used.

There is very little known about the Torok aging process. Very few have lived to seen Toroks age or die.

The Toroks' main goals seem to be domination of all life forms. Toroks are looking for an apparatus that will give them total power to control all of reality. Their secondary goals are the destruction of planets, galaxies, solar systems, and the enslavement of peoples with planetary resources that they can use.

The Toroks have established controlling galaxies throughout space. They are developing a technology that will allow them to travel to other dimensions and parallel universes, both past and future, with the goal of total domination of all life forms.

Toria is a highly technological advanced planet, utilizing all the resources and technology the Toroks have acquired from other planets and the people they conquer. They have technology that can destroy planets, energy power technology, stellar travel technology, intergalactic communications technology, advanced weapons technology, and knowledge of cosmic atoms manipulation.

The Toroks have developed a bio-suit armor that regulates their body temperatures. It allows them to exist in any atmosphere. It is used in the battles and invasions. It protects them from disease, and could withstand many powerful plasma and thermo- pulse blast. It is also near indestructible.

The Toroks also has mass weapons productions facilities on Toria and on their Torok colony outpost planets.

The Toroks utilize their conquered people as slaves to manufacture the productions until they invent a programmed computerized mechanical production line machine.

The Toroks population is innumerable. The women are warriors and scientists, and are in every field of advancement for Toria.

Although barbaric, Toroks are an intelligent and strategic people. They move together for one purpose and goal.

Toroks are characteristically very aggressive, warlike, relentless, domination driven, and considered a people that will destroy without compassion.

To be continued in

THE SUNDARIAN BOOK TWO
THE XANAIS ENTITY